CiCi RENO

#MiddleSchoolMatchmaker

KRISTINA SPRINGER

CICI RENO

#MiddleSchoolMatchmaker

KRISTINA SPRINGER

STERLING CHILDREN'S BOOKS

New York

STERLING CHILDREN'S BOOKS
New York

An Imprint of Sterling Publishing Co., Inc.
1166 Avenue of the Americas
New York, NY 10036

This 2018 edition published by Sterling Publishing Co., Inc.
Text © 2016 by Kristina Springer
Illustrations © 2016 by Sterling Publishing Co., Inc.

ISBN 978-1-4549-2863-8

Distributed in Canada by Sterling Publishing Co., Inc.
c/o Canadian Manda Group, 664 Annette Street
Toronto, Ontario M6S 2C8, Canada
Distributed in the United Kingdom by GMC Distribution Services
Castle Place, 166 High Street, Lewes, East Sussex BN7 1XU, England
Distributed in Australia by NewSouth Books
45 Beach Street, Coogee, NSW 2034, Australia

For information about custom editions, special sales, and premium and corporate
purchases, please contact Sterling Special Sales at 800-805-5489
or specialsales@sterlingpublishing.com.

Manufactured in Canada

Lot #:
2 4 6 8 10 9 7 5 3 1
03/18

sterlingpublishing.com

Cover design by Irene Vandervoort
Interior design by Andrea Miller

Cover photo Africa Studio/Shutterstock.com

To Maya and London, my own little yoga girls

Cici Reno @yogagirl4evr • 32 minutes ago
CHILD'S POSE - Kneel, drop your butt to your heels, reach forward. Head down and focus on breathing. Makes life's problems easier to handle.

Ugh. My nail polish is smudged.

I glance around for something to wipe up the blob of blue-green nail polish on the side of my toe. Spotting nothing else available on the pool deck, I decide to use my beach towel. There. Much better. Now it's back to work painting my toenails this rather awesome shade, Peacock Passion. A couple of girls from school, Madison and Alexa, are sitting together on the lounge chair next to me, watching and waiting for my response.

"Okay, so Brandy told Allison a secret that you told her not to share with anyone, ever?" I ask Madison. I keep my focus on my pinky toe. This one is always the most difficult to do.

"Yeah. And if she was *really* my best friend, she never would have told her. Now I don't know if I can ever trust

1

her again." Madison's voice shakes like she wants to cry.

"Right." I straighten up and wiggle my toes in the late-August sun. It's still warm and bright but not as aggressive as the July sunlight. Like it somehow knows that school starts in a week and it's thinking, *hey, gotta scale back the Vitamin D and ease these kids back into nine months of fluorescent light.*

I look over my nails carefully and, yep, this is the best shade of the summer. I grab my phone, snap a quick pic of my toes, and post:

> **Cici Reno** @yogagirl4evr • 0 seconds ago
> Winner! Peacock Passion. #25shades #summer #nails

I had carefully worked my way through Cici's Twenty-Five Shades of Summer, a nail polish schedule I'd set up the day after sixth grade ended, and wouldn't you know it, the very last shade I apply is my favorite. It's pearly and perfect, reflecting the water from the community pool like it knew it belonged here on my toes all along. But back to the problem at hand. Madison's BFF drama.

I set my phone down on my beach towel. "Okay, here's what I think, Madison. Brandy should never have told your secret. You're BFFs, and what she did was wrong. You need to tell her that."

"That's what I've been saying, too," Alexa pipes in.

"I'm not saying go all *Real Housewives* on her or anything. Just talk to her. Keep your tone light. Say, 'Hey, listen, Brandy, I told you a secret and it got back to me. I thought we were best friends, and that isn't cool. So if I'm going to be able to trust you, you just can't do that.' And then see what she says. Chances are, she'll feel bad and apologize."

Madison bites the corner of her bottom lip. "I guess I can do that. But should I stay friends with her? How do I ever trust her again?"

"Trust comes with time," I tell her. "Put her on a sort of secret friendship probation. Don't tell her your deepest secrets for the time being. Maybe after a while, say, three weeks, you test her with a small piece of information and see if that gets around. You can stay friends though. People make mistakes. Let the trust rebuild."

"You sound like a therapist or something," Madison says. "But I don't know. Brandy really hurt my feelings."

"Take Cici's advice, Madison. She's always right," Alexa says. "She's like a Magic 8 Ball."

I blow air in the direction of my toes. "Girl, I'm better than a Magic 8 Ball. You never have to ask me again later."

Alexa giggles and Madison nods. "Okay. Thanks, Cici. I'm going to talk to her."

"No prob," I reply. Just then, my phone buzzes. I glance down at it and see I have a new text message.

"I'M BAAAAAACK!!" it says.

I leap out of my lounge chair, knocking over the bottle of nail polish. "Eep! Aggie! Sorry, girls! Gotta run! Aggie is home from Florida!"

I pull my hot pink tube dress cover-up over my bathing suit and jam my feet into my flip-flops. I've messed up my nail polish job, but I don't care. My best friend is back from vacation!

I toss everything into my glittery peace sign backpack and race for my bike, which is locked in front of the park district pool entrance. Wait, I got so excited I forgot to text Aggie back.

I quickly text, "Yaaaaay! Meet @ Beanies in 15?"

"I'll be there!" she replies.

I hop on my bike and pedal hard toward Peony Lane Yoga Studio, my mom's business. It's only six blocks from the pool, in the same strip mall as Beanies. Mom opened it five years ago, and it's become a popular fixture in Bryerston. Ladies, and occasionally a guy or two, pop in daily for yoga classes, taught by Mom or one of her other instructors: Bonnie, Jackson, or Wendy. I love it there. I love my mom's soothing voice as she leads us through the poses, the calming music, and the smell of the burning incense. Yoga makes my muscles feel warmer, my mind feel lighter, and my problems seem easier. I always leave feeling more powerful than when I began. That studio is one of my favorite places in the whole world.

I barrel into the lobby, crashing into the antique wooden desk near the front. The giant blue vase of peonies shakes.

"Hey, slow it down, Cici," Mom says, steadying the vase.

"Aggie's back!" I say.

Mom grabs my hands and squeezes. "She is? Yay!"

"Oh, that's wonderful," says Claire, one of Mom's regulars. Claire just finished college and pops in for a class between job interviews. She says it helps keep her anxiety down.

"Aggie, you say?" Peg asks, sidling up next to Claire. Peg's in her standard biking shorts and pink "I'd rather be in Vegas" T-shirt. She's in her sixties, I think, but she can get into some yoga poses women half her age can't. She pours herself a glass of the cucumber water Mom always keeps out.

I nod vigorously. "I told her I'd meet her at Beanies in a few minutes, okay, Mom?"

"Of course. Give her a hug for me too." Mom's beaming.

"Thanks, Mom, I will," I say. I tear back out the door. Beanies is just seven stores down and around the corner. I run the whole way. As I approach the café, I spot Aggie facing away from me at an outdoor table.

"Aggie!" I yell and wrap my arms around her from behind. She leaps from her chair and throws her arms around my neck, and we jump up and down, squealing. "Oh my gosh, you're so tan and I think you're taller and . . . " Whoa. I pull back from Aggie. I know it's rude but I can't help staring directly at her chest. Her boobs are ginormous! When did that happen? "It feels like you've been gone forever," I say.

"I know, it feels like that to me too," she says. "We have so much to talk about."

"Soooo much," I echo and follow her into Beanies, glancing down at my own completely flat chest.

2

"**S**mall mocha, please."

"Switch your drink while I was away?" Aggie asks, accepting her iced tea from a second barista while mine rings up the mocha.

"Yeah. About mid-July. I thought about it, and vanilla steamers are very sixth grade, the old me. I've matured a lot this summer. I posted about it, did you see?"

"Hmm. I don't think so," Aggie says. "But I wasn't online much. My dad and stepmom are big on being outdoors. We were mostly at the beach. I pretty much only got on my dad's computer to email you and my mom. I did catch a couple of your cute nail photos though," she adds.

I grin at Aggie. It's nice to see my work was appreciated. My smile quickly fades when I notice a customer at the pickup counter leering at Aggie. I nudge her with my elbow and motion with my eyes.

Aggie follows my glance, sees what the guy is doing, and turns her face away.

He looks several years older than we are, maybe even in college. Yuck. And he's *still* staring at her.

I know I should stay quiet, but I can't. "Inappropriate much, guy?"

He looks at me in surprise, like he just noticed I'm here. "What?"

Aggie bites her lip and looks like she wants to crawl under a rock. I can feel my skin start to heat up with rage at this guy. "You're staring," I tell him. "Cut it out; it's creepy."

The barista looks concerned as she watches our exchange. I hand her my money and take my mocha.

"Wow, your little sister is kind of mouthy," the guy says to Aggie.

Is this joker serious? I feel my heart racing now. "Really?" I say. "I'm two months older than she is, actually."

He looks me up and down. "Dude, maybe lay off the coffee?" He smirks and chuckles as he picks up his cup and walks out of the shop.

We take our drinks and sit at a small table near the window instead of outside, just in case that guy is still out there. My pulse feels like it's beating in my ears.

From the way Aggie is staring down into her iced tea, I'm guessing she's totally embarrassed. Not that the whole scene was a picnic for me either. And something tells me it was just a preview of what's to come.

Aggie went away to Clearwater, Florida, for the summer, to stay with her dad and new stepmom. Most people come back from their beach vacation with a bag of shells or some sand in an empty water bottle, but Aggie's come back home with these giant boobs. Not that I can be mad at her for it. It's not like she can help her sudden summer growth spurt or that having boobs is bad. That would be like me having control over my light brown lackluster hair. But I have my eye on some Moroccan oil stuff to give my hair a little life. Maybe my next online campaign will test shampoos.

I think I'd better lighten the mood. "Hey, you reading tea leaves in there or something? Tell me if this is the year I finally get an *A* in science."

Aggie dips her shoulders, like she's trying to sink into her chair. "It keeps happening lately. I feel like guys are staring at me all the time."

I want to say something to make her feel better, to commiserate, but I have no idea how that feels. Nobody notices me. Everyone treats me like a little kid still, even though I'm twelve and three-quarters, practically thirteen. "Well, if you're asking my advice . . . " I pause and read her face to see if she wants me to continue.

She nods.

"If there are guys making you feel uncomfortable, tell them so. I'm not saying you have to get as loud as I was, but a firm, 'Stop staring at me!' wouldn't hurt."

"I'm not as good at that as you are. I have a harder time confronting people," Aggie says. "So far, I've just been looking at my feet, hoping the person would go away. It's worked okay, I guess."

"You can't let people treat you badly, Aggie. Just say 'Stop' if you can't think of anything else."

Aggie nods. "Okay, I'll try. And it's not just the guys acting goofy around me. My own mother completely embarrassed me at the airport. I was coming out of the gate and I see my mom. I wave and call out, 'Mom!' Well, her face screws all up like she saw a car accident or something and she blurts out, 'Oh my God, you have boobs!'" Aggie crosses her arms over her chest. "I could have died. Of course, everyone in the airport turned to look at me. I was so upset by all the attention. I was like, seriously? Boobs happen. Every day. All across the country girls are getting boobs. I'm not the first or last, so get over it."

"Did you really say that?" I ask excitedly.

"Nah," she says. "I just hurried over to Mom and tried not to make eye contact with anyone."

"Oh, Aggie," I say. "Well, don't you worry. We're back together now, and I'm not going to let anyone mess with you. If they try, they'll have to deal with all four-foot-nine-inches of me."

At this, Aggie finally cracks a smile.

3

Cici Reno @yogagirl4evr • 2 hours ago
BUTTERFLY POSE - Sit with your back straight;
bend your knees and bring the soles of your feet
together. Helps open your mind and heart. <3

"**A**s you come out of child's pose, I want you to move into dead man's pose," my mom says in her soft, instructor voice. "Savasana. Let go of your thoughts. Push aside any distractions of work or texts or emails you have to deal with. They will all be there later. Focus on yourself and the good work you did in class today. Take this time for you."

My favorite pose, I think. It requires you to lie still on your back for a while, eyes closed, palms up, and feet falling outward. And you just work on relaxing your muscles and focusing on your breathing. It's the best.

I'm glad I could catch Mom's last yoga class of the day. I really needed it. Seeing Aggie this afternoon left me feeling stressed, and I know it shouldn't have. She's the same old

Aggie, and I'm the same old me. I need to figure out exactly why Aggie's big boobs are bothering me so much and deal with it.

I decide I need a visual to help give my mind a break today and completely relax into the pose, so I focus on a large, beautiful palm tree blowing in the wind. Its leaves sway back and forth, and I can just about feel the breeze on my face. I'm concentrating on making my breathing even when *snap!*

The palm tree cracks in half and my eyes flicker open.

There's a minor disturbance near the door of the room. I sneak a peek at the large glass window near it and see Mom talking to my older brother, Luke, in the hallway. He's asking her something, but it's muffled and I can't hear them. And then I see *him* standing behind Luke.

Drew Lancaster. He catches my eye and smiles.

I gasp, completely messing up my breathing. Holy smokes, someone hit a growth spurt over the summer. Drew looks a few inches taller and also broader in the shoulders. The baby fat that used to fill out his face has completely disappeared.

Wait until Aggie sees him. She's been crushing on Drew since fifth grade. She's still mortified about the time we were at a family skate night for my brother's hockey team and she face-planted right at Drew's feet. He pulled her back up on her skates and asked her if she was okay. She just nodded. After he skated off, she told me that he was the boy she was going to marry. Of course, she was just being silly.

She'd never even spoken to him. But whenever we take her with us to a hockey game, she cheers for him the loudest. And when she doesn't come to the games, she'll ask me how her hockey boyfriend did.

Are Luke and Drew friends now? They've been teammates for years but never crossed into that "hang-out-at-each-other's-houses" friend zone. Will he bring Drew to *my* house? I have to tell Aggie ASAP so she doesn't drop dead of a heart attack if we come home from school one afternoon to find Drew sitting on my living room sofa.

Drew plays on the travel hockey team with my brother, and any time they have a home game, Aggie and I sit in the stands and totally check him out. The way his arms rock from side to side when he's racing down the ice, the bits of hair curling out onto his neck at the base of his helmet, the way he waves his hockey stick over the puck right before he shoots. He's pretty impressive. He can skate circles around lots of the guys, he's good at scoring, and when he checks someone, his victim sorta slow-motion slides down the glass, almost cartoon-like. He could totally go pro when he grows up.

Drew's never paid any special attention to Aggie though, aside from helping her up that night in fifth grade. And he certainly never noticed me. To him, I'm probably just Luke's little sister and nothing else. Just gawky and kind of small, more disregarded than desired, from a boy's point of view. Which I guess is true, visually, if you've only seen me and never spoken to me. I like myself well enough. But that thing about looks being deceiving is totally true in my case. My outside just hasn't caught up to my inside yet. On the inside, I'm heading toward high school, and on the outside, I'm just starting fifth grade.

Not that it matters at all what Drew thinks of me. Aggie called dibs long ago, and girl code states that you can't like a guy your friend likes. But maybe she wouldn't like him anymore. Maybe she prefers the shorter, pudgier-faced Drew of last spring. She's been gone all summer. Maybe her type has changed. Ah, who am I kidding? He's gorgeous. She'll definitely notice.

Luke and Drew leave, and Mom tiptoes back to the front of the room, trying to keep the disturbance to a minimum, but it's useless for me. It's hard to act dead when my heart is racing. Endless possibilities are running through my mind. If Drew and Luke are friends, he might start coming to family dinners or for ice cream. A family miniature golf outing or movie night. Will he sleep over? Oh my gosh, I might see him in his pajamas! Aggie will definitely want to hang out at my house even more if Drew's around.

The class empties out, and Mom and I begin wiping down the yoga mats. We pass the bottle of disinfectant back and forth while we talk.

"So, Mom," I begin. "Who was that with Luke? He looked sorta familiar." Haha, sorta familiar. You know, in that my-best-friend's-been-stalking-him-from-the-stands-for-two-years sorta way.

"That was Drew from hockey. Your brother went to his house to do some land drills. I wish he could have waited five minutes for class to end, though. He knows I hate having class disturbed."

"I didn't think it was *too* disturbing," I reply.

"Thanks for helping, Cici. I always get done cleaning up so much faster when you're here," Mom says.

"I like helping," I say.

"So tell me, was it great seeing Aggie again? How was her summer? I bet it was wonderful. Three months on the beach in Florida sounds glorious." Mom breathes in the warm yoga studio air like she's taking in a beach breeze rather than old sweat and cleaning solution.

"Um, yeah. It was good. She had a great time," I say, my voice suddenly mellowing out.

Mom stops wiping abruptly and tilts her head, studying me. "Hey, what's wrong? You two didn't get into a fight already, did you?" The worry wrinkles between Mom's eyebrows pop out.

A fight? No, Aggie and I don't fight. Well, almost never. There was that one time in sixth grade when we didn't talk for a whole week because she thought I was spending too much time with a new girl, Sabrina. I was just being nice, not looking for an Aggie replacement. It was torture having Aggie mad at me, and we promised we'd never let anything like that come between us again.

"No, no fight. It was great catching up," I say.

Mom doesn't look like she believes me. "Are you sure there isn't something wrong?"

Just your genetics, I think, and then mentally slap myself. Yikes, that was rude for me even to think. True, but rude. Mom's small-chested, which I guess is great for yoga. But I can see where this tiny train is headed, and things don't look good for me on the development front. It's not like I can say any of this to Mom, though. I can't tell her I'm jealous of Aggie without sounding silly, like the little kid I appear to be.

"I'm sure," I say.

4

Cici Reno @yogagirl4evr • 5 hours ago
WARRIOR POSE - Stand up straight with your left leg back and right knee bent. Turn your left foot out slightly. Raise your arms above your head and look up. Helps you to feel brave and confident when you are feeling meek.

Cici Reno @yogagirl4evr • 10 minutes ago
On the way to AWMS back-to-school bonfire! #AWMS #bonfire #soexcited

Cici Reno @yogagirl4evr • 5 minutes ago
Longest car ride ever #ugh #smoresdeficient

Cici Reno @yogagirl4evr • 10 seconds ago
Annoying older brother trying to dampen my #bonfirebuzz #wontwork #savemeahotdog

finish posting and slip my phone back into my pocket. It's near dusk when Mom pulls in the parking lot of Alton T. Wright Middle School. Luke's sitting shotgun, and I'm in back, as usual. Mom says even though technically it's almost legal for me to sit in the front, she still feels better if I sit in the back for a while longer, since I'm so tiny and all. Being small sucks.

"Do you guys need anything?" Mom asks. "Luke, take a twenty for you and Cici in case you want food or something. Or do you two want me to hang around for a bit?"

"No way. It's bad enough that you're dropping us off in front of the school in the minivan," Luke says. "I wanted to get out and walk a block ago."

It's the back-to-school bonfire, and absolutely everyone attends. It's a chance to swap class schedules, dish on teachers, and catch up on summer drama before class actually starts on Monday. Luke's an eighth grader this year, so he thinks he's a super big shot.

"True, sweetie, but then Mommy couldn't get a shot of you and Cici in front of the bonfire for the scrapbook," she replies.

Luke audibly gasps. "Mom!"

I giggle. She's totally teasing, and I know it.

"Fine, fine. Just give me a kiss and be on your way," Mom says.

"Good-bye, Mother," Luke says, popping open the passenger door and getting out. No kiss for Mom.

"Be out front by nine-thirty," Mom manages to yell just before the door is slammed shut. "What about you, Cici? Do I embarrass you to death too?"

I lean through the front seats and kiss Mom on the cheek. "Not yet, but you'll get there eventually."

The blacktop is packed. I head in the direction of the bonfire, which I can barely make out through the crowd, scanning for my friends. Aggie told me she'd meet me here. There's music blasting from a speaker somewhere, and small groups of friends are clumped together. Everyone seems giddy. Far away from the fire are a group of boys kicking a soccer ball around. Closer to it is a huddled group of what appears to be sixth graders assembling s'mores and shooting around nervous looks at the crowd. A bunch of boys to my right start chucking marshmallows at each other.

While I dodge a rogue marshmallow, I spot my friends Emma and London. We got close working on sets for the sixth grade play last year and we spent a lot of days lying out at the community pool this summer.

"Cici!" London yells, throwing her arms around my neck. "I missed you!"

I give her a squeeze back. She's so funny. It's only been two days since I last saw her. "Yeah, you've changed so much," I reply jokingly.

"Okay," she says, grasping my shoulders and suddenly sounding serious. "Casually turn your head and look toward the bonfire. But don't let anyone see you looking!"

I smirk. "How do I do that?"

She smiles. "Okay, fine. Just look. But be quick. Do you see him?"

"Who? *Adam*?" I say, drawing out his name. London has a monster crush on a tall, lanky boy named Adam. He hung out at the pool all summer too. We spent a good chunk of our time finding reasons to walk by his lounge chair.

"Shh! Someone might hear you," she says. "Of course I mean Adam. What's he doing?"

I take another look at him, and he's squatting near the fire. "Making a hot dog, I think. Actually, it looks like he's burning it."

London looks concerned. "Maybe I should go over and offer to help?"

"Yeah, do it," Emma says, and I nod.

"No," London says, shaking her head. "I couldn't do that. God, it'd be so obvious."

Emma and I look at each other and crack up.

"Did you come alone?" Emma asks.

I nod. "Aggie's meeting me here, though."

"Cici!" someone calls out and I look around to see who the voice belongs to. It's a girl from my gym class last year, and I wave. As I spin back around to talk to my friends, my eyes pause on my brother. He's talking to someone and laughing. Is it Drew? I stretch to the side to get a better look. I can't quite make out the profile, but it definitely looks like Drew.

Madison pushes her way through the crowd with Alexa in tow.

"Hey, Madison, Alexa. Having fun?" I say.

"Yeah, we already saw Mel, Anna, and Tony. Tony has a crazy haircut; wait until you see it," Alexa says.

Suddenly, our attention turns to a group of eighth graders counting loudly. "Eight, nine, ten," they chant.

"What's going on?" Emma asks.

"I think that big kid in the middle, the one with the creepstache, is trying to see how many marshmallows he can cram into his mouth," Alexa says.

"He has a mustache?" London asks in awe.

"Twelve!" the eighth graders scream, and a group of girls starts clapping. They're looking at the marshmallow eater like he's a celebrity. He bends over and spits, and marshmallows fly all over the ground.

"Ew," I say. My friends and I exchange a look and we all start giggling.

"I have to fill you in on what happened with Brandy," Madison says, tugging on my sleeve.

"Oh yeah. Be back in a sec," I say, and let Madison pull me a few feet away, into the crowd of seventh graders.

"So," Madison begins. "I did just what you said. I confronted Brandy."

"And?" I prompt.

"She burst into tears," Madison replies. "She felt awful about spilling my secret. And then I felt awful that she felt awful. She didn't try to lie or anything. She said it was a stupid thing to do and asked if I'd forgive her."

"What did you say?"

"I said I would. I mean, she came clean with it and didn't try to hide it or lie, you know? And I love Brandy. We've been BFFs forever. I want to believe her."

"Good," I say. "See, I told you it would work out. But ease

back into things. Don't tell her where you hid the bodies or anything like that."

Madison laughs. "I won't."

We make our way back over to our friends, and I see Aggie has arrived. "Hey, lady, we were waiting for you," I say to her.

I hold out my phone, and my friends and I instinctively group together and pose with the bonfire in the background. "Bonfire selfie," I say, and we all smile. *Snap.*

"My mom almost didn't let me come," Aggie says, rolling her eyes. "Drama."

"Glad you did," I say. Her mom is the anxious type— always getting worked up over one thing or another. I keep telling Aggie to send her to Mom's studio for some yoga. She needs it.

I'm posting the photo: Love my friends! #AWMS #bonfire when Emma says, "Aggie was just telling us about her summer in Florida."

I slip my phone back in my pocket.

"Yeah, it was weird seeing my dad married and all. But his new wife is really nice," Aggie says. "We hung out at the beach a lot, and she took me shopping a bunch of times. She's really into fashion. And we wear the same size, which is kind of weird, but cool, because she'd let me borrow cute clothes when we went out to dinner. It was kind of like hanging out with an older friend."

"She sounds cool," Madison says. "And I'm totally jealous

that you can fit into trendier adult clothes. I still have to get mine from the kids' department."

"Well, that's been about the only good part about this, um, situation." She waves a hand in a circle over her chest. "I really liked my new stepmom. But I'm glad to be home again too. I missed my mom and stepdad and my little brother, Henry. And you guys, of course. I feel like I missed a lot," she adds.

"We missed you too!" London throws her arms around Aggie's neck. "And don't worry, we can catch you up fast. For example, Adam is still really, really cute."

As London goes on about Adam, I casually scan the crowd again and find myself seeking out Drew. I find him easily, a few feet away from the bonfire, talking with Luke. And he's looking right at me. I put up one hand in a wave, and Drew smiles. My stomach flutters a bit at the attention. I smile back, pushing a loose strand of hair behind my ear. I try to catch Drew's eyes again and notice they're not quite meeting mine. Actually they're sorta going right over my head. I glimpse over my shoulder. It's just Aggie.

Wait, is Drew checking out Aggie? I should tell her. I whip my head back toward Drew, but the moment is gone. *They're* gone. Drew and Luke must have walked off somewhere, and I can't see them.

I cross my arms and sway slightly from foot to foot. Was Drew really just checking out Aggie? Or am I seeing things? He never paid any attention to her before. *Thank goodness Aggie wore her jacket to cover up a bit.*

Ack! Did I really just think that? Who am I? What is Aggie supposed to do, wear a parka for the rest of her life? This is just like the time at the beginning of sixth grade when Aggie's mom got her a smartphone, and my mom said I was too young to own such an expensive phone, despite my famous "flip is not hip" speech. I got a lot of likes after going public with that one.

I need to squash the jealousy. I think I need a yoga session *stat*. Some stretching and slow breathing would help me deal with letting go of the things I cannot change. Like a flat chest.

What I should do, as a good BFF, is tell Aggie that Drew was just checking her out.

I tug on Aggie's sleeve, pulling her a few steps away from the group. "Did you see Drew yet?" I ask her. "Doesn't he look . . . different?"

Aggie scans the crowd. "Where is he?"

"He was by the bonfire, talking to my brother. Let me see." I slowly spin around, eyeing the crowd. And then I spot Drew and Luke buying pops from a teacher sitting in a sports chair by a huge cooler. "There," I say and nod in their direction.

Her eyes land on Drew and she lets out a "whoa."

"He's even cuter than I remember," she says. "His hair is longer and blonder. And he's so tan. He looks like a surfer."

"You should talk to him. I just saw him checking you out."

"No way, he was?" Aggie looks shocked.

"Totally. Come on, I'll go with you," I tell her.

"I-I don't know. I mean, I want to, of course, but what if he doesn't like me?"

"Oh, he'll like you. Let's go." I march straight toward Drew, pulling Aggie by the hand. I stop in front of him, giving Aggie a final yank to join me. My brother glares at me, obviously not wanting to be seen talking to his sister. But we're not here for him, anyway. I wait for Aggie to say something.

And wait. And wait. But she's not saying a thing. Drew looks from Aggie to me and back to Aggie. *Awkward.* I give Aggie a light elbow to the ribs and plaster a big smile on my face.

Finally she opens her mouth to speak. "I, um, I . . . " she trails off.

Drew smiles warmly. "Hey."

Aggie looks frozen and her jaw hangs open slightly.

I clear my throat loudly. She quickly turns toward me, her eyes blinking rapidly. I give her an encouraging nod. *Just say hello*, I mouth to tell her.

I can feel my brother shooting daggers into the side of my face. But I ignore him.

Aggie turns back to Drew and wets her lips. "I mean, hi? Heh heh," she lets out in a nervous giggle.

"Having a good time?" he asks.

Aggie looks at me, and I motion with my eyes for her to look back at Drew. "Uh, fire, huh?" she says.

Well, this isn't going well at all. Drew's giving her a

concerned look now, probably because she sounds like she's having some sort of stroke. I have to save her.

"You're . . . tall," she adds.

Drew looks four or five inches taller than Aggie. So maybe around 5'9".

"Yeah," Drew says. He shifts uncomfortably.

Okay, time to step in. "Hey," I say. "Actually we just came over to talk to my brother."

"'Sup?" Luke says, annoyed at my mere existence.

"Can I have some money?"

I can feel Aggie nervously fidgeting next to me, spreading her gaze around everywhere, anywhere to avoid looking at Drew again.

Luke reluctantly gives me some crumpled-up and slightly damp-looking bills from his pocket.

"Thanks."

I quickly flip around, hooking my arm through Aggie's. I've got to get her out of here before she says anything else weird.

As we walk away, I hear Drew say to Luke, "Is your sister's friend okay?"

"Who cares?" Luke replies.

Ah, that sweet brother of mine.

Aggie covers her face in her hands.

I put an arm around her back as we walk. "It wasn't that bad," I lie to her.

5

Cici Reno @yogagirl4evr • 22 minutes ago
CRESCENT MOON POSE - Step forward with one foot into a lunge. Arms above your head, thumbs hooked together. Helps you follow your own path.

Cici Reno @yogagirl4evr • 15 minutes ago
Mountain-Salute-Fold-Half Fold-Plank-Chaturanga-Upward Dog-Downward Dog-Half Fold-Fold-Salute-Mountain #goodmorning #yoga #firstdayschool

The first day of school came too fast. I certainly did not miss waking up at 7 AM.

As I step into the shower after finishing my morning Sun Salutation, Luke pounds on the door, telling me to get out of the bathroom. Now that he's an eighth grader, he needs to spend twenty minutes staring at himself in the mirror, I guess.

I finish getting showered and dressed, taking my sweet time, and then head to the kitchen. I'm determined to grow a minimum of two inches this year, so I pour myself an extra-large glass of milk and fill a sandwich bag with granola for the car ride.

Dad comes in and pours himself a cup of coffee. "Did you brush your teeth?" he asks.

I roll my eyes at him. "Seriously?" Being a dentist, he's slightly obsessed with my teeth. But I'm in seventh grade now; I think I have toothbrushing under control.

Dad mimics my eye roll and in an ultra-dramatic voice he says, "Like, ohmigod, my dad is such a loser. He, like, totally cares about my dental hygiene. As if, gag me with a spoon, ohmigod." He takes a sip of his coffee and looks at me expectantly, smiling.

"I'm sorry, what language was that?" I ask him with a chuckle.

Dad laughs. "Mock me now but when you're the last of your friends in the nursing home to still have your own teeth, you'll thank me. Of course, I'll be dead."

I groan. "Not one of your 'when I'm dead' speeches. It's the first day of school."

Mom walks into the kitchen. "Todd, stop teasing her. Let's go, Cici," she tells me. "And grab your brother too, would you?"

"If I can tear him away from the mirror," I mumble.

At school, I make my way into the large auditorium with the rest of the student mob, scanning the room for Aggie, who promised to save me a seat. The stupid tag on my infinity scarf keeps catching on my necklace and driving me crazy. I need to find a pair of scissors and cut it out ASAP. I tried to dress maturely today, hoping I'd appear older. I've got on a plain white T-shirt, multi-color scarf, fitted jeans, and loafers. There's a pair of non-prescription vintage cat eyeglasses in my backpack that I haven't been brave enough to put on yet. Maybe by lunchtime.

I spot Aggie halfway up the right side of the auditorium and make my way toward her. "Hey, chica," I say, sliding into the seat next to her.

She flashes a nervous smile.

"What's wrong? First day jitters?" I ask.

She shrugs. "I don't know."

The principal adjusts the microphone and launches into his welcome back speech. He reminds us to pay attention in class and show respect to our teachers and peers. He's going on and on about what a great year it's going to be, and I can feel Aggie fidgeting beside me. I give her a sideways glance.

Aggie lowers herself down in her seat, her gaze shifting to the ground, and crosses her arms over her chest. I notice she's wearing an extra flowy top this morning.

A couple of boys three rows up are blatantly checking Aggie out. They're snickering and obnoxiously elbowing each other. Poor Aggie. What's equally obnoxious are the two girls sitting directly behind the boys. They're casting evil looks at Aggie and whispering loudly to each other, the kind of whispering that you intend for your subject to overhear. Yikes, this isn't good.

I slip my arm through Aggie's and whisper in her ear,

"Sit up, Ag. Be strong. They're just mean girls. Ignore them," I advise.

Aggie nods and sits up tall in her seat. "I know. I don't know why I let them get to me."

I stare directly at the girls, my face expressionless, until they're shifting uncomfortably in their seats and they redirect their attention to the stage.

"They're just jerks," I whisper to Aggie.

• • •

The rest of the morning flies by with English, science, and gym classes, and soon I'm standing in the lunch line behind Samantha Wexler. She's dressed very brightly with a hot pink and orange striped top and a matching bow in her dark hair.

"Hi, Cici, have a good summer?" she asks.

"I did," I reply. "How about you? Do anything fun?"

"Mostly just stalked R. J. Messick," she replies with a giggle. "Rode my bike past his house about a million times hoping to bump into him. Unfortunately, he still doesn't know I exist. Guess he's not too outdoorsy."

I laugh. "I'm sure he knows you exist."

"No, he doesn't," she says with a straight face. "I had my friend Audrey go up to him and ask if he knew me, and he said, 'Samantha who?' I'm totally invisible."

"Guys are oblivious. That's not your fault. You just have to make him know you. Do you have any classes with him?"

"Yeah, math," she says.

"Try to talk to him tomorrow. Say anything. Borrow

a pencil. Ask for a sheet of paper. Find out if you got the same answers for number five on your homework. Do that a couple of days in a row. Then try to figure out what he's into and bring that up in conversation. Like, if he's into football ask him who he's rooting for this year. Stuff like that."

"Yeah," Samantha says, a grin spreading over her face. "Those are all great ideas. Thanks, Cici! I'll give it a try."

"No problem," I reply, happy I could help. Some problems are easier to fix than others.

When I get home from school, I head straight for the kitchen to get an apple, and the thing that I both hoped for and dreaded comes true.

Drew Lancaster is sitting at my kitchen counter.

I freeze.

Luke is sitting across from him. Both boys have open laptops in front of them and are snacking from a bowl of popcorn in the middle of the counter.

"Hey," Drew says in my direction.

"Hey," I reply, giving Drew my best smile. I can't believe he's really here, in my house. Maybe I should hang around a bit and see what I can find out about him. There's no harm in getting to know him, and if I learn something that can help Aggie, all the better.

"Did you get homework already?" I ask him.

"Just a lame 'Intro to Me' piece for English."

"Ugh, that one?" I say, commiserating. "I swear at least one teacher assigns that every year."

"Yeah, seriously," Drew agrees.

I leaf through a pile of mail on the table, pretending I'm looking for something. Really I'm trying to make out the title on the spine of the novel poking out of Drew's backpack on the floor. I wonder if we like to read the same kinds of books.

"Did you want something?" Luke asks.

"Yeah. I'm thinking a snack. Maybe an apple," I respond, leaning on the counter. "Why, you want to slice it for me? That'd be sweet. No peel, please."

"Get it and get out," Luke says in an annoyed voice.

I narrow my eyes and shoot Luke an evil glare. He has zero reason to be annoyed with me.

Drew catches my scowl and smirks. "You guys are funny. I wish I had a sibling to bicker with."

"No, you don't," I reply.

"Yeah, yeah, yeah," Luke says. "Are you still here?"

"My parents work a lot so it's quiet at our house most of the time," Drew shares.

"Lucky," I say, heading for the fruit bowl. As I pass by Drew's laptop, he's updating his profile picture. He's shooting a puck outside, his hair blowing softly. He looks like Prince Charming on skates. His username is Drewlingmess. Hmm. I think I need to file this information away for later use.

"Okay, going now . . . " Luke says rudely.

"What's your problem? Did none of the girls at school squeal over your carefully coiffed hair this morning?"

A snicker escapes from Drew's mouth.

"I'm going to carefully coif your face if you don't get out of here," Luke says.

I stick my tongue out at Luke and turn to leave. Drew's smiling at me, and my heart skips a beat.

6

Cici Reno @yogagirl4evr • 19 minutes ago
WARRIOR 3 POSE - From Warrior 1, bend over
the top of your left thigh. Extend your right leg
behind you. Helps you be strong and fearless.

Drew's hot. And friendly. And he laughed at my jokes. I can see myself totally going for him, not that I ever actually would. For one, Aggie likes him. And everyone knows two best friends can't like the same guy. *If* they want to stay best friends, that is. And two, he's my brother's friend. Oh man, Luke would go berserk if I ever dated one of his friends! And three, Drew would never like me, anyway. I'm not his type.

I'm sitting cross-legged on my bed, staring at my laptop, where I have Drew's page up. Maybe Aggie could use the same advice I gave Samantha today. She can try to figure out what Drew's into and then have something to talk about with him. So the next time she's face-to-face with him, she won't fumble around for words. I bet I can learn a lot about

Drew by reading through his page.

Drew's such a nice guy up close and personal. I mean, I knew he was cute and a good hockey player, but having him in my kitchen, he's totally nice. He's not obnoxious like Luke and his other friends. He didn't tell me to get lost or anything. And it's not like I'm *that* much younger. Luke is only fourteen months older than I am, and Drew has to be around the same age. But that doesn't matter. I'm helping Aggie.

I scroll through his posts, trying to gather information on him. If I can just find out some of his likes, aside from hockey, then she'll have something to talk about. I can give her a list of conversation topics, and she'll be ready to say something clever the next time she sees him and without all the "uhs" and awkward pauses.

And then an idea hits me. What if Aggie talked to Drew anonymously? She could message him online and take her time forming her thoughts. Then he could get to know her slowly, and when and if they did meet up, she'd be way more comfortable. I grab my phone and call Aggie.

"Don't freak out, but Drew Lancaster is in my kitchen right now."

"What?" Aggie squeals into the phone. "He is?"

"Ow! And, yes. He's doing homework with Luke," I say.

"Oh my gosh, oh my gosh, you're so lucky! Sneak down there and see what he's doing."

"I was just down there," I tell her. "Besides, I have a great idea for you."

"What?"

"I have Drew's username. Message him. I mean, you don't have to say it's you. Just make up a name for now. Talk to him for a bit and when you feel comfortable, then you can try talking to him in person again."

"Cici, that's brilliant!" Aggie says.

"Thank you, I thought so myself. And, hey, I started a list of some of his interests so you can have something to talk about with him." As I say this, a tiny wave of jealousy comes over me. Aggie will start chatting with Drew, then they'll meet for coffee or something and fall in love. Then she'll have a great boyfriend, and I'll just have a lot of extra quiet time to myself. Maybe I'll start meditating.

"Wow, you think of everything," Aggie says. "It sounds completely perfect. Only one thing."

"What's that?"

"I can't talk to him, Cici! You heard me at the bonfire. I go from zero to dork in 2.3 seconds."

"But you'll be online," I tell her. "You can take your time typing, really form your thoughts."

"Yeah, I guess." She pauses. "Or *you* could talk to him for me. Please? You're so much better around guys than I am. Always so relaxed and cool. And funny," she adds.

If that's true, it's only because none of them ever want to date me. It's easy to be relaxed in that situation.

"I don't think so," I say. "It's weird."

"You couldn't possibly say anything weirder than I

would. Remember, 'uh, fire, huh'?"

I giggle.

"Please, Cici," she presses. "You know I would just be calling you every two minutes anyway, asking what to say."

That's true. "Okay," I reluctantly agree. "I guess it couldn't hurt. And Drew will never know, right?"

"Right, I'll never tell him. Thank you, Cici! You're the best!"

"Sure, sure, but hey, I'm not going to do this forever, you know. I'll just get you started. You'll have to take over at some point and eventually be able to talk to him in person."

"Okay, I will. Promise."

I hang up with Aggie and before I can give it a second thought, I create a new account for one SeraFrosted, a play on the character Sera Froste from James Dashner's *Infinity Ring*. From reading Drew's page, I can tell we share a love for the series and, hopefully, seeing my username, he'll be more likely to respond to me. I scroll through his posts until I find something we have in common.

Okay. Time to message Drew.

• • •

The next morning at school the five-minute-warning bell rings before our first class. Aggie's leaning against my locker, her books in her hands, when I get there.

"Hey, Aggie," I call. "Gee, I thought I was going to be so late. My mom drove about sixty the whole way here." I toss my books into my locker and grab my English book, the way-too-heavy anthology of English literature, and a notebook.

"Tell me everything! I'm dying," she says.

A wide smile spreads across my face. "We've made contact," I tell her, giddy to spill all the details this very second. I slam my locker door closed and hoist up my stack.

"No way!" Aggie squeals.

Just then a boy with shaggy brown hair stops in front of us. "Hi, Aggie, need help carrying those books?"

I survey Aggie's books and then frown at my own. My books are way heavier than Aggie's. Why doesn't Chumpy here offer to carry mine while he's being so generous?

Aggie's face quickly changes from excitement to annoyance. "No, thank you," she replies in a frosty voice. She's clearly getting more and more irritated with the unwanted attention she's been getting.

"Okay. Just thought I'd offer," he says. And Chumpy's out. He tears down the hallway like someone just said they're passing out free video games in the cafeteria.

I roll my eyes at Aggie. What a dork.

Aggie glares at his retreating back and then returns her attention to me. "So what happened? Did you message him?" Aggie asks, quickly recovering.

I pull Aggie down the hall toward our classes and out of the locker crowd. I check left and right to make sure no one is in earshot. "I talked to Drew online last night!"

"Oh my gosh, this is *so* huge."

"It's what you wanted though, right?" I ask, suddenly concerned. I mean, she begged me to do it.

"Of course," she says. "I asked you to." Her bottom lip juts out and her eyes look sort of sad. "It's just, I can't believe you really did. I mean, I guess I kind of wish I had been there to see it."

"Oh. I'm sorry, Ag. It was super brief, I swear." I bite my bottom lip and think of how I can fix this. "I've got an idea. Come over this afternoon, and we'll try to talk to him again. Together."

At this she perks up and nods. "Okay. But I can't stay long. I'm cooking dinner tonight."

"You are? Since when do you cook?"

Her eyes crinkle and her face brightens. "Since this summer. My dad loves to cook and he showed me how to make lots of dishes. Tonight I'm making spaghetti carbonara."

"Ooh la la," I say. "That sounds fancy. Microwaving my own vegan hot dog is the extent of my culinary skills."

Aggie laughs. "I'll show you some stuff if you want."

"Or you can just cook for me," I tease.

"That too. But hey, back to Drew. Tell me what you said. What did he say? Does he know it's me?"

"Not at all. I made up an anonymous name, SeraFrosted," I tell her.

"Who?"

We reach the door to my class, and I check the time.

"Ack, the bell's about to ring. I'll have to tell you the rest at lunch, but the important part is, I'm chatting with Drew."

"Right. Okay, every detail at lunch. If I make it until then. The suspense may very well kill me," she says, and takes off down the hall.

• • •

I'm sitting at this year's lunch table, waiting for Aggie. We picked it yesterday and claimed our territory. Not too far away from the cashier but far enough away from the nearest garbage can not to get pelted with food students toss out. The poor aim in this place is astounding.

I scan the room, hoping Aggie will see me and come to the table before she gets her lunch. I want to fill her in on everything before London and Emma get to our table. I don't want anyone to overhear our conversation. This would be really bad if it got back to Drew.

"I'm here, I'm here," Aggie says, sliding into the chair next to me.

"Great, okay, let me tell you quickly before the others get here. So I read through some of his posts and I was trying to figure out the best way to approach him so that he'd want to talk to me and not just think I was some random weirdo."

"That's good," she says, nodding.

"I made up a username and then I replied to something he posted, and then *he* direct messaged *me*!"

Her eyes grow wide. "I can't believe he sent you a DM that fast. After one little message?"

I shrug. "Well, he didn't suggest we run off to Tahiti together or anything. Just recommended a book I should read." I smile, recalling our conversation. "It's a start, though. I'm going to make him fall in love with me."

"Huh?" she says, her eyes narrowing slightly.

"Oh! And by 'me,' I mean you. Obviously." I let out an awkward giggle, and Aggie's face relaxes.

Just then, Emma and London sit down with their plates of chicken nuggets, and the conversation changes.

"From what I hear, Mr. Donovan doesn't even read the papers. He's just looking for word count. So, past the first page, you could type pretty much anything, and he'll give you an *A*," I tell her.

"Good to know," Aggie says, catching on quickly. "Ready to go get lunch?"

"Yeah, let's head up."

We make our way toward the lunch line, and suddenly a tall, lanky boy appears in front of us. "Hi, Aggie," he says.

"Hi," she replies cautiously.

"Want some of my cookies?" he asks. "They're double-stuffed." The table to our right explodes in laughter, and the boy exhales a laugh, spraying bits of cookie at us.

"Ew, you're gross," I tell him, pulling Aggie away.

When we're far enough away from the rowdy boys, I ask Aggie, "What was that?"

She shakes her head angrily. "Boys have been acting stupid all day. I swear I'm gonna lose it on the next one and get myself a detention. I wish they'd just leave me alone."

I give Aggie a sympathetic look. For the first time, I can't think of anything at all helpful to say. The boys are being obnoxious and the girls are acting catty and jealous. And Aggie hasn't done anything to deserve it. It's not fair.

7

Cici Reno @yogagirl4evr • 38 minutes ago
MOUNTAIN POSE - Stand with your feet hip-width apart, knees slightly bent, arms at your side. Be still. Helps you feel open and confident.

I roll out my yoga mat at the back of Mom's class. I've been racking my brain all afternoon, trying to figure out a way to help Aggie with her situation at school. I can tell it's becoming unbearable for her, but I don't want her to get in trouble by getting into a fight with anyone. Maybe all she can do is ignore it and hope it dies down soon. They'll have to get bored eventually. There are five minutes left before class starts, so I take a seat on my mat.

"Hello, dear," Peg says, walking toward me in the back of the room, with Claire two steps behind her. "Mind if we join you?"

"Of course I don't mind."

"Did you have a good day at school?" Claire asks. "Are they still serving that gross rectangular pizza?" She rolls her mat out next to mine and then does some shoulder rolls and neck rolls.

"Ugh, yes! It tastes like cardboard," I reply. "But otherwise school's good. The teachers haven't really started giving out too much homework yet."

"Eh, I always hated homework," Peg says, kicking off her shoes and setting them in her gym bag. "I always wanted to be outside, running around after school. Not cramped up in the house studying."

"Yeah, I guess," I agree.

"How are things with the BFF? I bet you two are glad to be together again," Claire says.

"Yeah, we are," I tell her. "Things are a little different this year. I mean, Aggie's changed some. But, yeah, I'm glad she's home."

"How's she changed?" Claire asks.

I try to think of how to describe Aggie's situation without being crude. "Umm, well, Aggie sorta blossomed this summer."

"Are they getting in her way when she's running or something?" Peg asks. She pulls on her matching green terry cloth wristbands and headband. She wears them at every class.

"Um, no, I don't know. I suppose they could be." I don't have them so I can't relate. "But the problem isn't with her, it's with everyone else. People are being kinda jerky to her."

"Ah, yeah. I know how that is. My daughter, Gwen,

developed early too. I remember those days," Peg says. She pulls off her socks and her toenails are pink glitter, which is so Peg.

"I wish there was something I could do to make her feel better," I say. "Or get everyone off her back. She seems so uncomfortable."

"Be her friend," Peg says. "Support her. Boys are teasing her because they're awkward and immature. Girls are mean because they're jealous. Kids are going to tease no matter what you do. If you're too tall, too small, too fat, too skinny. It's unfortunate, but it's been happening forever."

"People stink," I reply.

"That's true," Claire pipes in. "But not all of them and not all of the time. And Peg's right. Soon enough, the rest of the girls in your class will be developing, and Aggie won't be such a novelty. You'll see."

I nod, feeling a bit better.

Mom walks in and instructs us to get into an easy seated position for our opening mantra.

Class ends, and I can see through the window into the lobby where Luke and Drew are sitting on the couch, doing homework.

"Cici, tell the boys I'll be five more minutes," Mom says. "Just got to straighten up."

"Sure." I'm glad to have an official job to do, a reason to talk to Drew.

I head out of class and want to run up to Drew and

tell him that I checked out the book he suggested from the school library today, *The Last Token*. But then I remember that I'm me, Cici, and not the girl he met online. I'll have to wait until later at home to tell him. Instead I say what I'm supposed to say. "Mom said she'll be out in five minutes, then she can give Drew a ride home."

Luke grunts his response, not bothering to look up.

But not Drew. "Thanks," he says kindly.

"Sure," I reply, holding his gaze.

Drew doesn't act like he thinks I'm a pest or Luke's bratty little sister. He seems so cool. He'll make a great boyfriend for Aggie. Really great.

8

here's a knock at my bedroom door, and Aggie peeks
her head in.

"Get in here," I say.

Aggie rushes into the room, flinging her backpack onto
the floor. She grabs my flower-covered soft-top trunk from
the foot of my bed and drags it over to my desk to use as a
seat. "I'm so excited!" she says as she plops down on it. "Do
you think he's online now?"

"I don't know. Maybe. We dropped him off at home a
little while ago."

Her eyes widen. "You saw him?"

I nod.

"Lucky!"

"I was thinking," I start, "let's send out some random

posts so this SeraFrosted account doesn't look completely lame. I type:

> **Sera Froste** @SeraFrosted • 3 minutes ago
> The Drips are coming to town on tour this summer.
> #wannago #thedrips #gottagetthere
>
> **Sera Froste** @SeraFrosted • 2 minutes ago
> Up way too late reading #TheLastToken last night.
> #amreading #tired
>
> **Sera Froste** @SeraFrosted • 4 seconds ago
> My math homework is impossible tonight! #ugh
> #deathbyalegbra

Aggie screws up her face. "But I don't like reading. And our math homework was super easy today. I do want to see the Drips though," she adds. "Maybe we can get one of our moms to take us."

"Oh, it's just something to say," I tell her, bypassing the Drips comment for the moment. Though that's a great idea. I'll have to mention it to Mom later. "It doesn't have to be relevant."

As I'm trying to think of something else clever, I see my DM notice pop up. Ah! Is it Drew? I click it open.

> **D** Hey. Are you online now?

"Ack! It's him," Aggie says to me.

> Hey. **S**

> **D** Do you have time to chat?

I glance at Aggie. "Well, do we?" I tease.

Aggie wraps her arms around herself tightly. "Yes. Tell him yes."

So . . .

I place my fingers on the keyboard, ready to type, and turn to Aggie. "Okay, what do you think we should say?"

She shoots me a panicked look. "I don't know! You said you'd help me!"

"And I will," I assure her. "But what is something you might want to know about him?"

Aggie picks up a piece of paper off my desk and begins twisting it back and forth in her hands. Luckily it's not homework. "Um . . . " she hesitates, "ask him what he likes to do for fun."

I type in her question, and we wait.

"Why am I so nervous?" Aggie asks me, as she continues to choke the life out of my paper.

All kinds of stuff

Aggie wrinkles her nose. "Well, that's vague." She drops the paper back on the desk and begins to chew on her left thumbnail. "Ask him if he likes to cook."

No, but I like to eat. ☺

I giggle, but Aggie looks frustrated.

She sighs. "I don't know what else to talk about, Cici. I'm terrible at this."

"Let's ask him something about sports," I say.

I'm about to write "no, just yoga" when Aggie bolts upright in her seat and says, "Tell him I'm trying out for volleyball."

I cock one eyebrow at her. "You are? When did this happen?"

"I'll tell you in a sec. Just tell him," she urges me.

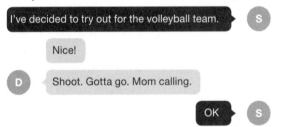

And he's gone. I turn to Aggie and grin.

She looks a little pale, like she might be sick.

"You okay?"

She exhales loudly. "I feel like I was holding my breath the whole time."

I giggle. "It's okay. It was just a chat, Ag. He doesn't even know who we are."

"I know, I know. I'm fine," she promises. "I was just really nervous."

"It'll get easier," I say encouragingly. "Hey, what was that stuff about volleyball?"

"Oh yeah." Her face lights up. "I've been meaning to tell you. I'm going to try out for the volleyball team this year."

"Wow."

She nods. "I played a lot this summer. My stepmom taught me. She played volleyball in college, so we spent a lot of time playing it at the beach. She's really nice. And she said I'm pretty good." Aggie shrugs but she can't hide her smile. "Mom, of course, is against it," she continues, the smile fading.

"Why would your mom care if you join volleyball?" I ask.

"She gave me a hard time when I brought it up. 'Is this like the time I bought you a viola and you quit orchestra after three weeks? Or when you begged for tennis lessons but would never practice because it hurt your arm?'" she says, mimicking her mom.

"That stuff was a long time ago. My mom would love me to join more school stuff. Did you tell her you're good at it?"

"Mmm, not exactly," Aggie says. "I didn't want to talk about what a great time I had with my stepmom. Like it would be rubbing it in or something."

"Doesn't she want you to get along with your stepmom?"

"Yeah, of course. I think. I don't know." Aggie shakes her head, and I can tell she doesn't want to keep talking about it.

"Well, I think it's a fab idea!" I tell her. "And I'll come to all of your games and cheer."

Aggie perks up. "Really? Thanks, Cici!"

"Of course. What are best friends for?"

Aggie gets to her feet. "I've really got to get home."

"Want my mom to drive you?" I ask.

"Nah, I rode my bike." Aggie reaches for the bedroom door and hesitates. "Drew seems cool, doesn't he?"

"Totally," I reply.

"And he's so cute. Don't you think he's cute?" she asks.

"Sure, he's nice-looking," I reply.

"Nice-looking? Are the Hemsworth brothers *nice-looking*?"

"Man, you've got it bad." Not that I don't agree. But I can't tell her that. "He's perfect for you, Aggie," I say, trying to convince myself and her at the same time.

"Really?" she says, sounding relieved. "I'm so happy to hear you say that. I mean, I've always liked him from a distance, but I didn't know if our personalities would really match up. But I trust you, so if you think we're perfect together, then I'm sure we are."

She trusts me. Why do I suddenly feel guilty? "Definitely."

"What about you?" Aggie asks. "You haven't talked about any crushes in a long time."

"Yeah, um, I guess there isn't a real 'Drew' for me right now. I don't know. Maybe someone will catch my eye," I say.

"Someone totally will, no doubt. And then I can help *you* get him."

Yeah, I don't see that happening. *Hey, really hot boy, stop staring at beautiful me and take a gander at my friend over here with the good personality.* No, thanks. But I say "Sure" anyway.

She flashes me a smile. "Now I really have to go. See you tomorrow."

After dinner, I go to my room and check the SeraFrosted account again. There's a message waiting.

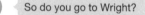

Before I can even think about it I reply:

Yes!

So do you go to Wright?

I had craftily followed a bunch of people from school that Drew follows so he'd think I was just someone from school rather than some random weirdo Internet girl.

Yeah. ☺

It's safe. He'll never figure out who I am. I'm just one of over five hundred students.

Have we met?

Hmm. I can't exactly answer that. I type back:

I'm not gonna lie, this is kinda fun. Talking to Drew, pretending to be someone else. On here, he has no idea what I look like or who I am, except for what I tell him. Not that who I am exactly matters anyway, since I'm doing this all for Aggie. But we do have some stuff in common. He loves to read, and I love to read. I make a mental note to fill Aggie in on that part of the conversation when I call her later.

We write back and forth for another ten minutes until my dad appears in my doorway. "Done with your homework?" he asks.

I minimize my window. "Just about."

"Finish up and bring it out to the living room so I can double-check it," he says.

"Okay, Dad." Once he leaves I type to Drew:

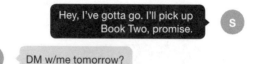

Hey, I've gotta go. I'll pick up Book Two, promise. **S**

D DM w/me tomorrow?

I can feel myself blushing even though no one else is in the room with me to see it. He likes me. I mean, Aggie. Me, being Aggie. At least enough to want to keep talking to me.

Definitely. Talk to you tomorrow. ☺ **S**

9

Cici Reno @yogagirl4evr • 32 minutes ago
FIVE-POINTED STAR POSE - Step feet wide apart.
Reach fingers out to the sides toward opposite
walls. Helps you feel open and energized.

'm not going lie, I've been looking forward to getting home and chatting with Drew all day today. A small part of me says that I shouldn't be, but I just push that part way down inside.

I check SeraFrosted's direct messages and there's one waiting.

> **D** 23.

Hmm. I type back:

> 23 what? **S**

Drew writes back immediately.

> **D** Oh good, I was hoping you'd be online now.

> What about 23? **S**

> 23 is the number of times I listened to The Stall song you told me I had to hear. And . . . didn't hear a thing. Nothing unusual.

I giggle. The Stall is my all-time favorite band. I have pictures of them up all over my room. The other night I was telling Drew that during their song, "Frozen Tunnel," if you listen really closely you can hear a low gravelly voice speaking over the guitar solo. The lead singer claimed in a magazine interview that they didn't lay any vocals over that part and that it was a mystery how it got on there. Like a ghost or something.

> Maybe you're just not tuned into the spiritual world.

> And you are? See any dead people now?

> LOL, no. Maybe I'm just more open. Or have better hearing than you do anyway. ☺

> I do have a vampire gnome statue on my bookshelf.

> Um, why???

> Joke present from a friend. What, you have no strange belongings?

I settle back onto my pillow with my laptop on my knees.

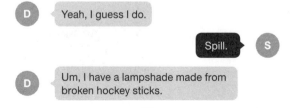

> Yeah, I guess I do.

> Spill.

> Um, I have a lampshade made from broken hockey sticks.

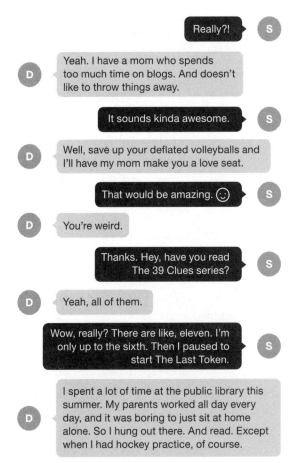

S: Really?!

D: Yeah. I have a mom who spends too much time on blogs. And doesn't like to throw things away.

S: It sounds kinda awesome.

D: Well, save up your deflated volleyballs and I'll have my mom make you a love seat.

S: That would be amazing. ☺

D: You're weird.

S: Thanks. Hey, have you read The 39 Clues series?

D: Yeah, all of them.

S: Wow, really? There are like, eleven. I'm only up to the sixth. Then I paused to start The Last Token.

D: I spent a lot of time at the public library this summer. My parents worked all day every day, and it was boring to just sit at home alone. So I hung out there. And read. Except when I had hockey practice, of course.

Oh. Suddenly I feel a minor ache in my chest. Drew was alone all summer? Did Luke know? We should have had him over more. He didn't have to be on his own. I don't know what to say so I just type:

S: Wow.

D: It was fine, I love to read. Did you get the second Last Token book?

> **S** I did! Picked it up on the way home. I was reading it right before we started chatting.

> **D** Oh, did you want me to let you go read?

> **S** I didn't say that.

> **D** ☺

> **S** ☺

I can feel my own face grinning so hard, my cheeks feel like they might pop. Neither of us types anything for a few moments.

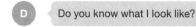

> **D** Do you know what I look like?

Uh-oh. He's fishing for information. Does he know I know him in real life? I have to think of a clever reply that doesn't give too much away.

> **S** Well, I can see your profile pic.

There. Truthful and doesn't give anything away.

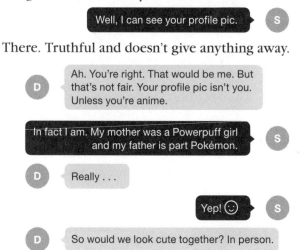

> **D** Ah. You're right. That would be me. But that's not fair. Your profile pic isn't you. Unless you're anime.

> **S** In fact I am. My mother was a Powerpuff girl and my father is part Pokémon.

> **D** Really . . .

> **S** Yep! ☺

> **D** So would we look cute together? In person.

Ugh. Drew! I know what he's trying to do, what he's hinting at. At least I think I do. He's trying to move us offline. Only I'm not ready for that. I'm not ready to just turn him over to Aggie and end our conversations. Not yet.

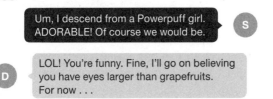

Um, I descend from a Powerpuff girl. ADORABLE! Of course we would be.

LOL! You're funny. Fine, I'll go on believing you have eyes larger than grapefruits. For now . . .

His last two words echo in my head. *For now.* Our relationship can exist online for now, but at some point, and maybe soon, I'm going to have to pass him off to Aggie. I take a deep breath, count to four, and exhale slowly.

10

Cici Reno @yogagirl4evr • 58 minutes ago
HAPPY BABY POSE - Lie on your back and hook your big toes with your index fingers. Rock side to side like a happy baby. Helps you feel calm.

The next day at school, I feel like I'm positively radiating. Like I just got a pumpkin facial, a basket of kittens dropped off on my doorstep, and a giant mint chocolate chip ice cream sundae all in the same day. I even posted first thing this morning:

> **Cici Reno** @yogagirl4evr • 32 minutes ago
> Nothing can bring down my mood today! #giddy #sohappy #goodmorning

I know, everyone hates vague posts, but it's not like I could scream my true thoughts from the rooftops. I'm happy. And it's all because of Drew. We chatted for over an hour last night and he's just so sweet and smart. I have no clue how he can be friends with my brother. Most of Luke's friends are smelly, belching, obnoxious troll-like beings that need to take their shoes and socks off to count to twenty. Well, except for Luke's friend Matt—he's missing a toe. But Drew, he's so different. He's kind, he reads a lot, he likes music, and he's really funny.

Yeah, so I've got a teensy little crush on Drew. We get along so well! It's fun, it's harmless, and no one will ever know. It's not like Aggie can get into my head and see what I'm thinking. I'll play it cool. I'm doing this for her after all. It's not like he'd ever like me in a million years. Aggie's the one who has a real chance. With my online game and her looks, we're a great package.

I'm at the cashier, paying for my lunch and already regretting my choice of meal. The lunch lady behind the counter said it was a chicken burrito, but it looks more like a wet lump of clay the art teacher would toss on a desk and instruct us to transform into a pot. It's gray and on the soggy side. And that's the outside of the burrito. Who knows what the inside is going to look like.

I take my change and head for our lunch table, bumping into Aggie on the way. "Hey, Aggie," I say cheerily.

"You're in an awfully good mood," she says.

I nod. "It's my happy day. Nothing can bring me down," I tell her.

"Anything specific happen?"

"Nope," I reply quickly. "Just feeling good. Are you getting hot lunch today?"

"Nah," she says. "I brought a salad from home."

I fill Aggie in on a few of the highlights of last night's awesome conversation with Drew as we make our way to the lunch table. There are some things that I don't want to tell her though, almost like I want to keep them private between Drew and me. Personal stuff, like what he told me about being alone all summer. Which I know is completely weird. But still I keep it to myself.

"There's one other thing I should tell you," I begin. "I think he's trying to move on to the next step."

Aggie stops walking abruptly and looks at me. "Seriously?"

I nod. "Yeah. He was trying to get a visual on what you look like. Don't worry, I dodged him for now. Unless you're ready for that, of course." I hold my breath. *Please don't be ready, please don't be ready*, I chant in my head.

Aggie's eyes dart around the lunchroom. Almost like Drew is going to pop up from behind a beam or a garbage can. "Do you think I'm ready to talk to him face-to-face?"

I panic. If she takes over the relationship, then Drew and I stop talking. "Um, well, do you feel ready? I mean, if you're still not sure, I can talk to him a little more online. You know, to really hook him for you."

She considers this and then her face relaxes into a smile that looks like relief. "Okay. It sounds like you're doing great making me sound good."

"Yeah," I agree, feeling incredibly guilty.

Madison and Alexa are already at our table when we

arrive so I clam up on the Drew talk. "Hey, girls," I say.

"Hi," Alexa says. "Sit, sit, you're just in time for Madison's story about science class."

"Okay," Madison begins. "So Mrs. Barnwall is up at the SMART Board opening up an exercise she wants us to do, right? And while she's not paying attention, Tony gets up and takes one of the lab mice—Squirt, I think it was—out of his cage and—"

Just then London arrives at our lunch table and plops down on a chair, sighing loudly.

We all glance at her and then Madison continues her story. "So, like I was saying, Tony takes Squirt and opens up the cabinet at the back of the room where Mrs. Barnwall keeps her purse. Absolutely everyone is watching him, right?"

"Gah!" London says loudly. She lets her head fall back, and her arms drop to her sides.

Aggie and I exchange glances.

Madison gives London a slight frown but continues, "Only instead of putting Squirt in her purse, he drops him on the floor, and everyone in class starts screaming."

London folds her arms on the table and dramatically drops her head onto them with a *thunk*.

"Long story short, Mrs. Barnwall had to call the janitor in to catch the mouse," Madison says quickly and then turns to London. "All right, what's your deal? Are you sick or something?"

London slowly lifts her head and nods. "My life is over."

We lean in, and Aggie puts a comforting arm on London's shoulder. "What happened?"

"It's Adam," she says, her voice wobbly. "I just saw him holding hands with . . ." she takes a deep breath, "Katie St. James." She drops her head into her hands.

"Oh no," Alexa says, covering her mouth with her fingers.

We all exchange devastated looks. London has it bad for Adam. This has to be breaking her heart. I know I would be upset if I saw Drew holding hands with someone. I mean, on Aggie's behalf. I think.

I rack my brain for something to say that will make London feel better and quickly realize there isn't anything that will do it. She sure doesn't want to hear clichés about there being other fish in the sea or what-have-you. All we can do is be there for her.

"I'm so sorry, London," I say as I get up and make my way over to her side of the table. I wrap my arms around her and squeeze. "This really, really sucks. You've got us, though."

Madison, Alexa, and Aggie get up and join us in a group hug.

"Cici's right," Aggie says. "We're here for you."

I smile at my best friend and feel another wave of guilt. I definitely don't want to be the one who causes her to have a broken heart. I need to reign in my feelings. And quickly.

11

Cici Reno @yogagirl4evr • 17 minutes ago
PLOW POSE - Lie on your back; lift legs over your
head and try to touch your toes to the floor. Helps
you appreciate a new point of view.

The minivan is crowded with Mom, Dad, Luke, Aggie,
me, and Luke's huge, stinky hockey bag. I don't know
what he does it with it, but it always smells like he's lugging
around a dead body. Why do hockey players *refuse* to wash
their gear? It's disgusting. We're on our way to watch Luke's
hockey game, and Aggie's spending the night. I can't wait to
have an hour and a half of uninterrupted Drew-staring time,
where no one can question me or think I'm weird because
hey, I'm watching the game. Or at least one particular player
in the game.

We're dressed for the cold stands. I'm wearing a navy
and white striped sweater and a navy knitted cap, and
Aggie's got on a long sleeve pink shirt with a really cute
turquoise scarf carefully wrapped around her neck. There's

still some time until the first period starts, so we head for the lobby to check out the video games and hit the snack bar for a hot chocolate.

I'm kicking butt on an old pinball machine when I hear Drew clear his throat right behind me. I miss the ball completely and I lose. I spin around and am just inches away from him. "Oh! Hi, Drew," I squeak out, completely freaking out on the inside. What if he can tell just by looking at me that I've been the one chatting with him online?

"Hey," he says easily.

Okay, he's not letting off any vibes that he knows it's me. Calming down now.

"Shouldn't you be getting ready for your game?" I ask. Not that I'm not jumping-out-of-my-skin happy that he's standing here talking to me. He's so, so cute all dressed up in his hockey gear, his blue eyes sparkling. I haven't been this close to him when he's been dressed for a game before and he looks gigantic. Which makes me feel even smaller.

"Yeah, I came out to fill up my water bottle." He turns his attention to Aggie and flashes her a heart-stopping smile. "Hey, didn't I see you at the school bonfire?"

Whoa. For a moment I forgot Aggie was even here. Or that I'm the one trying to get her and Drew together.

Aggie turns a deep shade of red.

"Yeah," she replies softly. "I'm Aggie."

Drew seems completely taken with Aggie, and it's like I vanished right into thin air. "Yeah, Drew," I say. "Aggie's my best friend. She's in seventh grade too. Like me."

Aggie turns her head away, seemingly nervous.

I give Aggie a look, waiting for her to say something else. She's really going to have to get over this shyness if she ever expects anything to happen with Drew. But she says nothing.

"Well, we were just about to go get some hot chocolate to bring back to the stands, so good luck in your game," I tell him. I slip my arm through Aggie's and drag her toward the snack bar.

"Nice meeting you, Aggie," Drew says to our backs. I toss a glance over my shoulder and see him bite the corner of his lip as he watches Aggie go.

● ● ●

It's the middle of the third period and the score is four to one, Drew having scored two of the goals. He's looking right in our direction in the crowd. I glance at Aggie, and she's staring straight down at her lap.

"Aggie," I say in a low voice so my parents don't overhear. "Can't you see Drew is totally checking you out? You're going to have to be able to talk to him at some point if you're really interested."

"I am interested. But maybe I'm not ready," she says. "I'm too nervous and he's too cute, and when he's right there in my face like that, I just can't do it. My mind goes blank."

I nod. Maybe it's for the best. Maybe she should just forget all about Drew.

"That's why it's so great that you're helping me by talking to him online," she continues.

Okay, I guess Aggie won't be forgetting about Drew just yet.

The game ends 4-2; Luke and Drew's team gets the win. How we survive the car ride home with Luke's disgusting hockey bag stinking up the car, I'll never know. I want to hang my head out the window like a dog to get air. Luke, of course, finds it amusing and keeps trying to push it toward me. He's so annoying. Thankfully, Aggie's sleeping over tonight, so Luke will stay far away from us for the rest of the evening.

Aggie and I are in my room, playing around with my makeup case. She's trying to create a "smoky eye" on me but it looks more like a smudgy mess.

I check myself in the mirror. "Ack, I'm scary looking! I can't believe people go out in public like this."

Aggie laughs. "Well maybe I did it wrong. Want me to try again?"

"Nah." I reach for a makeup wipe and start cleaning the goop off my eyes.

Aggie's staring at my laptop. "So, how many times have you talked to him?" she asks.

"Drew?" I stop wiping my face, suddenly nervous.

"Yeah."

I don't want to tell her the truth. "Um, not much. We've briefly chatted, like, three or four times now." Suddenly I want her far, far away from my laptop. I don't want her to pull up our conversations and read everything we've been writing. I know I shouldn't feel this way, but I do.

"Wasn't it so weird seeing him today, though? Like, he doesn't have any idea that you are the girl he's chatting online with."

"Oh yeah. Kinda. But he's not going to find out. I mean, I'm doing it all for you."

"But what if it turns out he really likes you and not me?" she asks.

I let out a laugh. "That's one thing you'll never have to worry about, Aggie. Drew would never like me like that in person."

"You never know, he might," Aggie says.

I shake my head. "I don't think so. He sees me plenty in person, and I can tell he doesn't think of me as anything other than Luke's little sister. Sure, he's nice to me and all. He's never rude or anything, which makes me wonder how he's even friends with my brother. But yeah, I don't think he'd ever look at me in . . . that way."

There's an uncomfortable silence in the room.

"Not to mention, he's *your* guy," I add. Maybe I should have made that point earlier.

Aggie shrugs. "I don't see how he'd ever really like me anyway, considering how strange I act any time he comes within five feet of me."

"Of course he likes you! I can tell. The way he looks at

you? It's really obvious. If you stop staring at the ground, trying to avoid his eyes, you'll notice next time," I kid her.

A smile spreads across her face. I can tell I reassured her. "Listen," I say. "I'll start giving you details of everything we talk about online. And then you'll be ready with something clever to say the next time you see him."

"Yeah? What kind of things do you guys talk about?" Aggie asks.

"Oh, all kinds of stuff. Books, TV shows, hockey, music. We were even talking about Mr. Adwell, the gym teacher. Did you know he's dating the school librarian? Guess he's been checking out more than books."

"Ewwww," Aggie says. "They're both like, a hundred years old."

"Senior citizens need love too, Aggie. Don't judge." At this we both burst into giggles.

"Oh my gosh, oh my gosh." Aggie's wiping tears from her eyes. "I just keep picturing her in those long prairie skirts and clogs she wears all the time and him with his short shorts and whistle. And then it cracks me up all over again!"

"Stop, okay, stop, you're making my side hurt!"

It's good to laugh.

"Okay, it's your turn for a makeover. Have a seat," I tell Aggie, nodding to my desk chair. I pick up my eye shadow kit and set to work.

12

> **Cici Reno** @yogagirl4evr • 41 minutes ago
> TRIANGLE POSE - Stand feet apart. Bend, touch
> the ground with one hand, and reach up with the
> other. Helps you hold it all together.

We dropped Aggie off at home earlier this afternoon, and all of my homework is done for Monday. I go online, looking to see if Drew has written. Talking with him has become more and more comfortable. We really are starting to be friends. If I can't have him in real life, this is definitely the next best thing. Although, if I'm going to be truthful with myself, I know it's only a matter of time before I don't have this anymore—this anonymous cyber relationship thing we have going on. Eventually Aggie will get over her nerves when she's talking to Drew and he'll see how gorgeous she is, and then they'll fall in love and that will be it. I'll be back to just my everyday life. But for now, I'm just going to enjoy any little bit of him I get.

I check my direct messages, and I have a note waiting

from Drew. I type a quick hello and a message immediately pops up from him.

> There you are 😊

> **D** I just happen to be online right now. Not stalking you at all.

> Okaaaaaaay, that's good to know, I guess? **S**

Him stalking *me* is funny.

> **D** Really, I swear I'm normal. Though you probably know that. You know me already right?

> ???? **S**

Gah! I don't know what to say! If I admit I know him, then he'll think I'm some weirdo tracking him down on the internet. Which I am, but he doesn't need to know that. It's for a good cause.

> **D** I think you know me. Which isn't fair because I have no clue who you are. Unless your real name happens to be Sera. Kind of doubt it though. 😊

Aw, man. At least he's still smiling though. I've got to try and switch the subject.

> How was your weekend? **S**

> Pretty good.

> We won our hockey game.

> **D** I scored two goals.

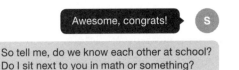

> Awesome, congrats! **S**

D > So tell me, do we know each other at school? Do I sit next to you in math or something?

He's not going to let this go. Why does he have to know who I am? We're getting along so well semi-anonymously. Aggie's not ready to talk to him in person yet. And I can't let him find out Sera is really me. He'd probably be all mortified and then go tell Luke, *Dude, your little sister is harassing me online.* Then Luke will tell Mom and Dad, and probably other kids at school, and I'll be humiliated on a global level. He can NOT find out who I am! But I've got to say something.

> No, I mean, no we don't sit by each other in class or anything.

> But yeah, I know you. Well, I've seen you.

> We're not like friends or anything. **S**

D > Ouch. I'm hurt. We're not friends?

> I mean in real life we're not friends. You're totally my online BFF! **S**

D > I really don't know you?

Why is he making this so hard?

> No, I don't think so. Not really. **S**

D > Meet me.

I gasp. You know that feeling when you're home alone and no one is supposed to be home for hours, but then you hear a big *thud* in the basement, like someone is in the house, and you're completely frozen in place with sheer panic? Yeah, that's what's going on right now.

D You still there?

I look down at my hands, willing them to type, but they're totally shaking.

Um, what? **S**

Meet me.

D Why not? We get along great. Let's meet.

Oh man. Well, this is it, I guess. Aggie has to take over. I pick up the phone and call her. It goes to voicemail. I'll have to stall him.

No, I don't think so . . . **S**

D Why not? Do you have a boyfriend?

No, it's not that. **S**

D Do you have a third eye in the middle of your forehead? A long fluffy tail?

I smile at the screen.

Ha! No, my parents had the tail removed when I was a baby. **S**

D Then meet me. This weekend.

The smile flees and panic sets back in. This weekend? Is he kidding?

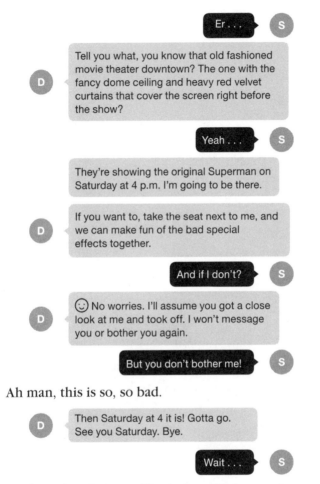

S: Er . . .

D: Tell you what, you know that old fashioned movie theater downtown? The one with the fancy dome ceiling and heavy red velvet curtains that cover the screen right before the show?

S: Yeah . . .

D: They're showing the original Superman on Saturday at 4 p.m. I'm going to be there.

D: If you want to, take the seat next to me, and we can make fun of the bad special effects together.

S: And if I don't?

D: ☺ No worries. I'll assume you got a close look at me and took off. I won't message you or bother you again.

S: But you don't bother me!

Ah man, this is so, so bad.

D: Then Saturday at 4 it is! Gotta go. See you Saturday. Bye.

S: Wait . . .

But he's already gone. That's that. We have a date.

13

Cici Reno @yogagirl4evr • 9 minutes ago
PYRAMID POSE - Arms behind your back, press your fingers and palms together. Step one foot forward and bend. Helps you be strong and bold.

Drew hasn't written me again, and I'm completely freaking out. I thought maybe I could reason with him, convince him we didn't need to meet and could just continue with our online relationship. Or maybe tell him I have to spend the weekend with my sick grandma. Impromptu trip to the lake. Anything. But he's not responding. He's forcing me into a corner. Meet him, or no more chatting. We gave him a ride home from hockey practice yesterday, and I swear, I was dying the entire time. He and Luke joked around, talking about something that happened in gym class, and I spent the ride staring out the car window, feeling like my face was on fire. He has absolutely no interest in me, Cici, Luke Reno's little sister, sitting two feet away from him in the back seat.

And Aggie knows something is up because I was acting super weird all day. But I couldn't tell her at school and risk a meltdown. I asked her to meet me alone for coffee after school. I have to convince her it's time for her to take over and meet up with Drew.

I'm sitting at our usual table in Beanies, practicing my deep breathing until Aggie gets here. Inhale slowly through the nose, exhale loudly out my mouth. And repeat. I catch an older boy giving me a look over his laptop.

"What?" I snap. "It's called breathing. I'm trying to calm down."

He raises his eyebrows. "Doesn't look like it's working."

I shake my head. "Whatever," I mumble. I close my eyes and take another slow breath. I don't know why I'm so nervous. I'm not the one who has to see a movie with Drew on Saturday. Though, if things were different and I could go as myself, I'd love to.

"Hey, Cici," Aggie says.

My eyes pop open and I see her slip into the chair at our table. "Hey, Ag."

"So I talked to my mom again about trying out for volleyball next week," Aggie says. "It took some doing but I convinced her to let me try out. I had to promise it wouldn't interfere with schoolwork or family time, AKA, babysitting Henry."

"Really? That's great! I'll go with you to tryouts and cheer you on from the sidelines," I offer.

"You will? That would be great. I think you'll keep me calm."

"Of course I will. If things start to go badly, I'll pull the fire alarm to disrupt the whole tryout. That way you'll get a second chance," I add.

"Wow, that's super nice of you. And not at all illegal," she teases.

"No problem at all. What's a tiny misdemeanor for a friend?" I need Aggie in a good mood for what I'm about to tell her.

"So were you working on homework?" Her eyes gloss over my books sitting on the table.

"Um, no, not really. I was pretty much just waiting for you, so that we could, you know, talk."

"Yeah, you've been acting strange all day. So spill." Aggie slips her jacket off her shoulders and onto her chair, shaking her long blond hair. I catch that same boy who was giving me grief about my breathing checking out Aggie.

"Well . . . " I pause, biting my bottom lip, ". . . how do I say this?"

The bell hanging over the door to the café rings, and a mom with two small children head for the counter.

Aggie tilts her head and furrows her eyebrows. "I'm listening."

I nervously tie a stray straw wrapper into knot after knot. "You sorta have a date on Saturday . . . with Drew."

Aggie shrinks back from me and her mouth falls open as

she registers what I just said. "What? No! No way. I told you I'm not ready!" She swings her hand out to the right, sending a container of sugar substitutes flying. We both turn to see the yellow packets flutter to the ground. Before either one of us can bend over to pick them up, the teenage boy has collected them all and is handing them back to Aggie.

"Here you go," he says, giving her an awkward smile.

She nods at him. "Thanks."

We both watch him take his seat, and then Aggie turns her attention back on me. She leans in and says in a hushed voice, "You know I sound like a huge idiot each time I'm near him."

"But you knew that I was only talking with him online to hook him for you and that you were eventually going to take over and talk to him face-to-face," I tell her.

"Yeah, when I was comfortable." She points to her face, which is now the color of a blushing tomato. "Do I look comfortable?"

Her eyes look kinda wild, and I feel bad for her. "Well, it's sort of a now or never situation."

"What does that mean?"

"Drew said I, well, *you*, need to meet him this Saturday, or he's done talking to me . . . us. For good." I bite my lip. I hate the idea of never getting to chat online with Drew again.

Aggie shakes her head, staring hard at the table. "I just don't think I can do it. Maybe we should forget the whole thing. Maybe I'm not ready to date. Maybe in a couple of years . . . "

A couple of years? But Drew is here now.

"It's not like you'd have to *date* date," I say quickly. "It's just a movie. He wants to put a face to the words, know who he's been chatting with. You can always stall him and say your parents won't let you date or something, if you want to take things slow. I can keep talking to him online. I don't mind." *Really*, I don't.

"How would I even know what to talk about?" Aggie finally asks.

I'm suddenly filled with a rush of relief. This is going to work, and Drew isn't going anywhere. "That's the beauty of going to a movie," I say hurriedly. "You don't have to talk. And I can prep you with a couple of things to say just in case you do chat a little. And I can go to the movie too, sit way far in the back, and if you get stuck, you just excuse yourself to the bathroom and come and ask me whatever it is."

"You really think he won't be disappointed that it's me?"

She's got to be kidding, I think. "No, not at all. Does this mean you'll do it?"

Aggie gives me a forced half-smile. "Yeah, I'll do it."

Cici Reno @yogagirl4evr • 23 minutes ago
SIDE ANGLE POSE - From Down Dog, bring left foot next to left hand. Bend left knee and bring your right hand next to your left foot. Twist to the left. Lift left hand straight up and let your gaze follow. Helps you release sadness when your feelings have been hurt.

'm in the very back row of the movie theater in an aisle seat, completely in the dark. My hair is in a tight braid and tucked under a baseball cap. I hope this will mask my identity. Drew is sitting about fifteen rows ahead of me, calmly chomping away on a small popcorn. How is he so relaxed? I'm completely freaking out back here and I'm not even on their date! Aggie's waiting just outside of the theater for the movie to start. She wants to talk to Drew as little as possible and thought this would cut down on the chatting. Which is kind of perfect. She'll seem aloof and he will probably be even more intrigued. But what if she bails at the last moment? Maybe I need to go out there and give her a little shove.

The movie begins and Drew strains his neck, looking

around to see if his date is coming. I hunch down low in my seat, not wanting him to see me. The theater is pretty full, so I think I'm safe. Aggie enters the theater and stumbles a few feet from me, but catches herself before she falls. She shoots me a panicked look and I give her a thumbs-up. I can see her put one hand on her chest and take in a deep breath.

Ah! This is it!

Aggie approaches Drew and plops down in the seat next to him, sending his phone flying off the armrest. He quickly retrieves it and even though I can only see the side of his face, I can see a look of surprise and then a smile of recognition. That's a good sign.

Aggie shifts uncomfortably in the seat, and Drew offers her some popcorn. She takes a handful and then focuses on the screen. Drew returns his gaze to the movie, but I can see him sneaking sideways glances at Aggie. He's totally into her, I can tell.

I settle back, trying to feign some interest in the last days of Krypton playing out across the screen in front of me, but it's impossible. I can't take my eyes off the back of Aggie and Drew's heads, looking for signs that they're getting along. They're both just watching the movie. This really was the perfect way to meet Drew. It's impossible to have a real conversation since everyone around you will *shhh* you if you try to talk. But just on the off chance he did get chatty, I wrote a list of topics on the palm of Aggie's hand with a black marker.

CHAPTER FOURTEEN

Oh wait, Drew's leaning in toward Aggie and whispering. What's he saying? Aggie's head falls back. She's laughing. Maybe he made a joke. I wonder what it was. I hope Aggie remembers so she can tell me. Now she's whispering something back to him. I told her to try not to say much of anything, let him do any talking, and just nod every so often. But she looks like she's not stumbling over her words or anything from the look on Drew's face.

Now Drew's laughing too. He's covering his mouth, trying not to be too loud. Whatever she said must have been really funny. It's a good thing that they're getting along like this. Really good. Yep. It's awesome.

So . . . why am I filled with a horrific amount of jealousy right now?

I want to be up there sitting with Drew, hearing his jokes, and eating his popcorn. But that's impossible. Aggie has dibs on Drew. She's the one who has had a crush on him for forever. True, she doesn't know him like I do since we've been talking so much. But she'll get to know him. Now that they've broken the ice, she can ease into taking over the relationship. I'm happy for her. Really. She's my best friend.

Deep breath, inhale through the nose, exhale out the mouth. Okay, I can handle this. I need to just relax, sit back, and try to enjoy the movie. Soon it'll be over and I can get out of here and not have to watch Aggie and Drew together.

The movie is nearing the end and I sneak out of the theater before the lights come up. Aggie and I agreed that when the movie ended she'd say a quick good-bye to Drew and then meet me in the ladies room. I pace the sticky bathroom tile floor, occasionally slapping on the hand dryers for noise. After what seems like an eternity, but is probably more like fifteen minutes, Aggie rushes in.

The first thing I notice is, Aggie really is very pretty. She curled her hair today and she has on a touch of eye makeup and pink lip gloss. He cheeks are a little red too, probably from all of the excitement. How could Drew not fall for her? It'd be impossible. I plaster the biggest smile I can muster on my face. I want her to know I'm super happy for her and Drew.

"Oh my gosh, Cici," Aggie says hurriedly. "Did you see us together? I can't believe I really just did that! It was horrible!"

"What? How?" I sputter, totally confused. From where I was sitting it looked anything but horrible.

"I completely messed up!" she wails. "I just know I sounded like an idiot. My hand got greasy from the butter and then I couldn't read my notes. And he was asking me questions about some CD or something and I said I liked to listen to rap, and he said I thought you hated rap and . . . ugh. It was awful."

"No, Aggie, you're not seeing what I was seeing. Drew totally likes you. I could tell by the way he kept sneaking peeks at you when you weren't looking," I say.

Aggie sniffles. "Really?" she asks, sounding hopeful.

"And I was thinking he likes you, not me."

"Me?" I spit out, shocked. "Why on earth would he like me?" My heart is beating so hard I can feel it in my ears.

"No, I mean, he likes *you*, Sera Frosted. He kept accidentally calling me Sera. 'Want some popcorn, Sera? Want me to go get you a pop, Sera?'"

"Oh, Sera. Right."

"Yeah, and then he was asking me stuff like, 'Did you really build an Eiffel Tower in Minecraft and how did you do it?' and I was all, oh no! No clue what he was talking about so I said, 'I'll tell you later, this is my favorite part,' trying to get him to refocus on the movie. It was crazy," she says.

"Do you . . . think you'll go out again?" I ask hesitantly.

"I don't know," Aggie says. "It was awkward."

"It was only the first date. I just need to prep you better next time. I should have told you about the Minecraft stuff. I'm sorry," I add.

"He asked if he could have my phone number so we could text or he could call me. And I panicked for a sec but then said, 'Oh, I can't technically date until I'm sixteen and I'm not allowed to text boys. My mom reads my texts so I can't give you a number.' I told him we'll just keep chatting online like we've, I mean you've, been doing." She checks my face. "That's okay, right?"

"Oh yeah, no problem," I tell her. "I can keep chatting with him."

Aggie walks toward the bathroom door. "So do you

think the coast is clear? Can we get out of the bathroom?"

I had told my mom that Aggie and I were watching the movie together and asked if she could pick us up around seven PM in front of the theater, giving Drew enough time to clear out. "You better be the one to check the lobby, just in case. We don't want him to see me here."

Aggie peers out into the lobby. "Yep, he's gone. Let's go hang out in the arcade until your mom gets here."

I follow her out the door. I can still feel my adrenaline pumping. I can't believe our plan really worked.

• • •

Back at home after dropping Aggie off, I head straight for my room and my laptop, dying to see if Drew has written me yet. I know it's a bit silly to think he'd rush right home and message me after seeing Aggie only an hour earlier. But he could have. Unless he doesn't actually like her. Maybe Aggie's not his type at all? Maybe he'll never write me again? Oh, who am I kidding, of course Aggie's his type. All the boys like Aggie.

I log on and gasp. There *is* a message there. Why am I so nervous? It's not like *I* just spent the afternoon at the theater with him. Well, not that he's aware of anyway.

> Hey Aggie, can I call you that now? LOL.
> Thanks for seeing Superman with me today.
> I had fun.

I immediately start to type back but then stop myself. It looks too eager to respond right away, doesn't it? Don't boys like when girls play hard to get? I stand up and walk around my room, straightening things up. I pick up a few pieces of clothes that missed the hamper and toss them in. The framed poster of a medieval castle on my wall is crooked and I realign it. I log out of my SeraFrosted account and sign into my regular YogaGirl4Evr account. I have a message asking me what the hardest pose I still haven't mastered is. I reply:

> **Cici Reno** @yogagirl4evr • 0 seconds ago
> Eight-Angle Pose is SO hard. Can you do it? #notyet #yoga

I sweep up the pile of change off my nightstand and drop it into the head of my light-up Yoda bank. "Mmmhmm, smart saving your money is," the Yoda voice in my bank says to me, just like it does every time I add money to it. I giggle. I was just telling Drew about my bank a couple of days ago. He said it sounded cool and was going to hunt one down for himself. Drew, Drew, Drew. Okay, that's enough time. I race back to my seat, sign back into the SeraFrosted account, and type frantically at the keyboard.

I had so much fun too. <3 Superman. Great flick.

What about the guy sitting next to you . . . ?

He was ok too 😊

I'm practically giddy getting to chat with Drew again like this, but I have to keep reminding myself that I'm just doing it for Aggie. It makes no difference how well we get along online. I need to keep my feelings under control and just help my best friend get the guy who's perfect for me—I mean, her.

> **D** I couldn't believe YOU are SeraFrosted.
>
> Is that bad or good?
>
> Disappointed? **S**
>
> **D** What? No, not at all. I just met you at my last hockey game is all. Were you there checking me out?
>
> No, I wasn't. **S**

I type that fast. We don't need him thinking Aggie's a stalker.

> I was there with my best friend, Cici. I've gone to a bunch of her brother's hockey games with her. Guess you never noticed me. **S**
>
> **D** Right. Luke's little sister. I hadn't seen you before.

Ouch. Luke's little sister. I knew that's all he thought of me. A lump forms in my throat. I don't know what else to say. I just stare at our open Direct Message box, the cursor blinking at me, waiting for me to write anything at all.

> **D** I liked seeing you now . . .

I half-smile at my screen. That's nice of him to say, I guess. Even though it isn't me he's seeing.

You're very pretty, Aggie.

Ugh. I wish he'd stop calling me that. And the more he goes on about how he thinks me, Aggie, is pretty, the worse I feel about the real me, Cici. I think I better stop typing for now. I'm not in the right frame of mind for this.

Hey Drew, I gotta run. Message you later. S

D ????

I close the window and slap the laptop shut.

15

Cici Reno @yogagirl4evr • 23 minutes ago
LOTUS POSE - Sit cross-legged. Right foot on your left thigh and vice versa. Helps you to feel balanced when you're feeling off-balance.

I didn't write to Drew at all yesterday or today. He probably thinks I'm mad at him, and in the tiniest of ways, I am. Though I have no right to be. He didn't do anything wrong. He now knows I'm Aggie and he likes me, "Aggie." Our plan came off without a hitch. Technically things are going great.

So why do I feel so awful?

I'm walking to lunch with Aggie, talking about our American history paper due next week on the French and Indian War. Mr. Lito is letting us work on it in pairs, and we're trying to figure out when we can get together to write it. Neither of us is paying close attention to where we're walking and we crash right into Drew. My books go flying out of my hands.

"Whoa," I say. "Where'd you come from?" I bend down

to collect my stuff. Drew also squats and swoops the rest of my stuff into his arms.

"Sorry about that. Here you go," he says, handing me my books.

"Thanks," I say. He's talking to me but his eyes are clearly on Aggie. I glance at her and her cheeks are completely flushed and she's staring at her feet.

"Hi, Aggie," he says.

"Hey," she mumbles, still not looking at him.

Yikes, this is bad. Why didn't we think that we might run into Drew at school? Well, because there aren't many eighth graders who come all the way down to the seventh grade hallway, for one. Usually each grade sticks to their end of the school. Drew had to come all the way over here searching for me, I mean, her, us, whoever.

"Is something wrong?" He gives her a curious look.

Which she'd see if she'd just look up at him. I softly give her an elbow in the side.

"Oh, um, what?" Aggie fumbles. "No, everything's great. Thanks."

Drew looks at me and I grin. Absolutely nothing strange going on here.

Yeah, right.

"Uh, okay, then." He returns his gaze to Aggie and leans in. Softer now he says, "You haven't written me in a couple of days."

"I haven't?" she asks.

I clear my throat loudly.

"I mean, yes, I haven't. Sorry. I'll write you tonight," she adds, looking at me for confirmation.

She did not just do that. I quickly divert my attention to my history book and start picking at some gummy leftover tape in the corner. Sheesh, Aggie, don't ask for my permission to write to Drew! That won't look fishy or anything.

"Um, cool. Okay, I gotta get to math," Drew says slowly. "Later."

"Okay, bye then," Aggie says, looping her arm through mine and yanking me down the hall toward the cafeteria.

I glance over my shoulder and catch Drew giving us a puzzled look. Ugh. Not good. We're definitely going to have to work on our routine to avoid this kind of situation again in the future.

"See? See?" Aggie hisses in my ear as we're fast-walking through the swarm of students in the hallway. "What did I tell you? I open my mouth and *blech* comes out. Can you feel my pulse? It's racing a mile a minute. What did I even say? I'm such a loser."

"No, it's fine," I tell her. "Honestly, It's not as bad as you think. I would have prepped you if I thought he'd hunt us down at school." I check over my shoulder again to see if Drew is still lingering there, but he's gone. I wonder what he's thinking right now.

I don't wonder for long since there is a message from Drew waiting from me when I get home.

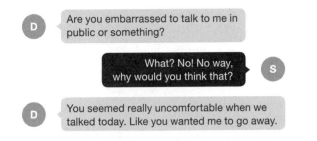

D: Are you embarrassed to talk to me in public or something?

S: What? No! No way, why would you think that?

D: You seemed really uncomfortable when we talked today. Like you wanted me to go away.

Well, yikes. That's sorta true. We did want him to go away. But only because we weren't prepared.

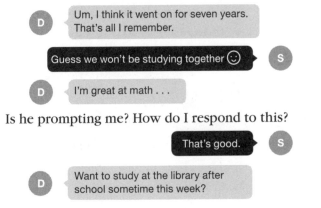

S: No, I was just surprised to see you. That's all. Cici and I had our heads together, talking about the French and Indian War and then you were suddenly there.

S: I don't suppose you remember much about that war from last year's history class.

I add in the second message, hoping to change the subject.

D: Um, I think it went on for seven years. That's all I remember.

S: Guess we won't be studying together 😊

D: I'm great at math . . .

Is he prompting me? How do I respond to this?

S: That's good.

D: Want to study at the library after school sometime this week?

Um, noooooo. We very much do not want to meet again this week. Aggie needs more prep time before we try this again.

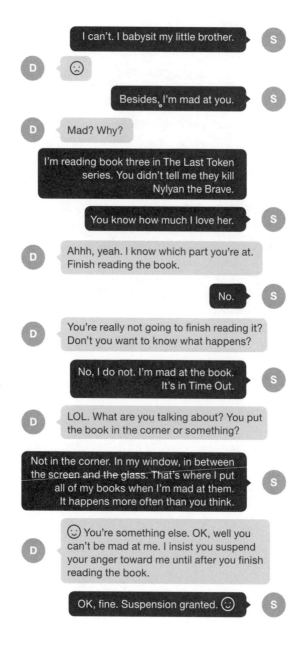

I smile to myself too. This. This is the Drew I love talking to. Now, if we could just manage to keep things going online and avoid any more face-to-faces, all would be good. On my end, anyway.

16

Cici Reno @yogagirl4evr • 32 minutes ago
TRIPOD POSE - Kneel and place crown of your head on the mat. Place your hands on the ground in front of your face. Place your right knee on your right tricep. Place left knee on your left tricep. Helps you find a new outlook when your world has been turned upside down.

It's Aggie's turn to serve again, and she nails the volleyball right over the net. No one on the other side gets even close to returning it. She's got a crazy strong serve. I've never even seen her play volleyball before, but she's definitely a natural.

I'm sitting in the stands of the school gymnasium, partly watching Aggie try out for the volleyball team and partly trying to organize the notes for our American history paper in my lap. I told her I'd take the lead on the paper since she needs to concentrate on tryouts. She's a sure shot to make the team. All the other girls look amateur next to her. She must have practiced a ton over the summer. I give my legs a quick stretch in front of me. I haven't been to Mom's yoga class in two days and I'm really missing it. And I won't have time to make it tonight either, since I'm here with Aggie. I had just about mastered a tripod headstand last week and I don't want to lose my gains. I definitely have to take a class tomorrow.

I'm jotting a couple of sentences down about the Battle of Jumonville Glen, which is thought to have launched the French and Indian War, when I distinctly get the feeling someone is staring at me. I look at the court, and Aggie is giving me one of those wide-eyed, panicked looks. But why? Is she suddenly freaking out about her tryout? Kind of late, since she's smack-dab in the middle of it. I glance around the gym, trying to locate what could be setting her off, when I see him. Oh no. How did he know we'd be here?

Drew is standing in the corner of the gym, watching the tryouts.

What do I do? Aggie needs to concentrate, not have an anxiety attack. What's he doing here anyway? Didn't I tell him I, Sera/Aggie, was busy this week? Drew turns like he's going to leave and then suddenly stops, spotting me.

Uh-oh.

He starts climbing the bleacher steps in my direction, and now I'm the one totally panicking. Breathe, breathe. I suck up as much air through my nose as I can and let it out mouth in a huge sigh. Ugh, didn't help. He's still marching straight for me. What does he want with me anyway? Me, Cici? I'm Luke's little sister. I'm not anyone to him. He can't possibly have anything to talk about with me. No way he figured out it's me talking to him online, right? Impossible.

Oh man, he's gonna sit down next to me. I'm going to hurl.

"Hey, Cici," Drew says casually.

"Hi, Drew," I squeak out, and then a huge swoosh of air escapes me. I didn't even realize I had been holding my breath, which is a huge no-no in yoga. I usually have better control than this.

He plops down next to me, putting his feet up on the step in front of us. I hug my history notes to my chest for support because I'm feeling slightly swoonish, and wouldn't that be just my luck to faint here in the school bleachers in front of everyone. While 95 percent of my body is completely flipping out at my current predicament, having Drew Lancaster sitting next to me, wanting to talk to *me* about who knows what, I'm aware of the 5 percent of me thinking, "Yay! Drew Lancaster is sitting next to me in the school bleachers! How do we look together?"

"Is it okay if I talk to you?" he asks.

Really? Is it okay if *he* talks to *me*? Here, let my series of cartwheels across this row of bleachers be your answer! Ah, there's that 5 percent piping up. And with the return of the other 95 percent, I am quickly filled with dread and want to crawl under the bleachers and hide until he goes away.

"Um, sure," I force myself to say instead. "What's up?"

"Well, this is going to sound weird, but word around school is you're pretty good at giving advice and stuff. And I just thought maybe you could give me some."

Advice? He wants my advice? It's usually the girls asking

me for advice. I'm kinda flattered that the guys must be mentioning me too. Maybe I have a career ahead of me as a psychotherapist? An online advice columnist would work too.

"Oh yeah. I guess I'm okay with advice-giving. What's the problem?" I glance at the volleyball court and Aggie has resumed volleyball tryouts. She dives for a ball and manages to return it.

He hesitates and then turns his face toward me and lowers his voice. "It's Aggie." I can feel his breath on my cheek, and the hairs on the back of my neck stand up. "I, I can't figure her out."

I'm a bit dizzy from sitting so close to Drew and I can feel my pulse picking up its rate. "Um, what do you mean? Aggie's Aggie."

Drew scoots a little closer and checks the court for Aggie. His thigh accidentally bumps mine, and I jump. "Sorry," he says.

"Oh, what? No, no biggie." I try to recover. Does he notice how flushed I am? Ugh, I hope not.

"She's sort of sending me mixed signals," he continues. "Like, she's really great online when we're chatting. We talk about so much. She's cool."

I curl my toes in my gym shoes. Awww! He thinks I'm cool! I can't help it, a smile creeps across my face.

"But in person? She acts sort of strange. Like she doesn't know me. Or doesn't like me. I don't know," he adds quickly, shaking his head. Drew's backpack is leaning against his knees and he's twirling one of the straps around and around his finger. He must be nervous too.

"Oh no," I say hurriedly. "I'm sure that's not it at all. Aggie can just be . . . shy sometimes. That's it."

"She won't talk to me on the phone or text or anything," he continues.

"Her mom won't let her text boys," I say, recalling what Aggie told me she had said to Drew the day of the movie date.

"Yeah, she mentioned that. But—this sounds crazy, I know—it's just, it feels like she doesn't want to see me. At all. Like, she avoids me if I run into her at school. She won't meet me to hang out or anything outside of school. She'll only talk to me online. It's like, she only likes me when she doesn't have to look at me. I just don't get it." His voice cracks with this last statement. I can hear some hurt there, and it about kills me.

This isn't good. I don't want Drew thinking I/she/we don't like him. Just the opposite! I glimpse Aggie on the court and she's giving me a puzzled look. We have to fix this. I know she may not feel completely ready, but she needs to go on another date with Drew or he's going to know something is up.

"You know what?" I say to Drew. "Ask her out again. Online when you're talking," I quickly add, suddenly fearing he'll march down to the court and ask Aggie out right now and completely wreck her tryout. "Aggie can be super-shy, but I'm sure she's warming up. She definitely likes you. She'll go out with you for sure."

"Really?" he gives me a hesitant crooked smile and my heart melts. He looks so unsure of himself right now, and I just want to give him a big hug.

"Definitely."

Drew stands up, looking much happier than he did a few moments ago. "Thanks for the talk, Cici. It helped," he says with a nod.

"Sure," I say and watch him bound down the bleacher steps and out the gym door.

Okay, this is it. Aggie needs to talk, really talk, to Drew. And in person.

17

Cici Reno @yogagirl4evr • 39 minutes ago
PLANK POSE - Prop yourself up into a push-up position, keeping your back straight. Helps you to feel strong and positive.

We're sitting on Aggie's bed with our backpacks in between us. Aggie's mom invited me over for dinner, and since Mom is still teaching classes, she said that was fine.

"So when are you going to tell me what the scene with Drew was about?" she asks.

"You were so, so good at tryouts today. I think they should make you captain. Your serves were amazing."

"Yeah . . . " she says.

"And that color purple looks really good on you. Totally brings out your eyes," I add.

"You're stalling, Cici . . . " she starts.

"You're so pretty, Aggie. And so nice. And such a great friend. And—"

"Cici . . . " she warns. "Tell me what you and Drew were talking about at tryouts. No more flattering. Is it bad?"

I force a laugh. "Of course it's not something bad. It's actually great."

I get off the bed and walk over to her closet. I push tops to the left, looking them over.

"Really? What?" she asks.

I yank a sparkly emerald green top from her closet and hold it up to myself. "Is this new? It's adorable."

"Cici!" Aggie snaps.

"Okay, okay," I say. I rehang the shirt in her closet and fall cross-legged onto her beanbag chair printed with pink owls. "He did want to talk to me about you. He thinks you're acting weird."

"He does? I knew it," she says, shaking her head. "He thinks I'm a freak."

"No, he doesn't think that. It's just, you act like you don't want to talk to him whenever he sees you."

"I get flustered," she answers quickly.

"Yeah, I know, I told him that. I said you're just shy."

"I don't even know what to say to him when he comes up to me. I have no connection with him, Cici. You do," she says.

"Try to act natural. Make a connection. He thinks you don't like him. He sounded really hurt," I tell her, feeling the pain in my heart return.

"Ah geez," Aggie says, twisting her lips. "I don't want

to hurt him. We should have never started talking to him. I told you I wasn't ready."

"I know, but we were already in too far to turn back at that point. And besides, he really likes you. And I know how we can fix this," I add.

"How?" she asks.

"Go out with him on another date."

"Oh no," she says, "I'll just screw up again."

"You just have to really talk to him, face-to-face, without distractions. And you wouldn't have to meet him in private, Ag. What about a public place? Somewhere you're comfortable? Like Mama Rosa's Pizzeria?" I suggest. Mama Rosa's is in the same strip mall as Beanies and Peony Lane. There's a small dining room in the front of the restaurant if you want to sit down to eat, and a counter for people getting takeout. Aggie and I have been going there for years. I can see her thinking it over.

"You think I can do it?" she finally asks.

"I really do," I quickly tell her. "I'll even be there with you. Hiding, though, of course. If you get stuck, you can just ask me whatever it is. I won't let you mess up, I promise."

She lets out a heavy sigh. "Okay, let's set it up."

• • •

After dinner Mrs. Miller gave me a ride home. Mom wasn't home from the studio yet, and Luke and Dad were plopped in front of the TV, eating sub sandwiches and watching a baseball game.

"Hungry, Cici?" Dad asks, holding out a sandwich to me.

"No thanks, Dad. I ate with Aggie's family."

Luke tears his eyes away from the screen to glance at me. "Yeah, Drew said he talked to you today at school."

I feel my back stiffen. He told my brother?

His eyes drift back to the TV screen. "He likes Aggie, I guess. Don't know why he's bothering with a seventh grader though."

"Drew's in love? Are they going to go steady? Will she wear his varsity sweater?" Dad teases.

"What? No," I quickly reply. "They're not in love. Well, I mean, they're just talking."

Luke starts cracking up. "What are you even talking about, Dad? No one wears varsity sweaters."

"You got any other friends for Luke, Cici? I think your brother is feeling jealous and wants a girlfriend of his own," Dad says.

"No, I don't," Luke says, playfully swiping at Dad's shoulder. "Especially not any of Cici's friends."

"None of my friends would ever like you anyway, you big bubble butt," I tell Luke. I head for my bedroom, wanting to get away from Dad and Luke and this whole conversation.

"This butt is all muscle, I'll have you know," Luke calls after me, and Dad is laughing hysterically.

"Yeah, so is your head," I yell back as I slam my bedroom door. Dad and Luke always act like kids whenever Mom isn't around. It's so annoying.

I drop my stuff on the floor and head over to my laptop to see if Drew is online. It's interesting to know that Drew has been talking about Aggie to Luke. He must really like her, me, whoever, to actually be talking about us to my brother.

There's a message from Drew waiting for me when I log on.

D Hey, you looked great at tryouts today. Hope you make the team.

Thanks!

Me too. Love volleyball. S

Even though I don't love it and Aggie does.

D Did your book ever come out of time out?

Yes! I finished it. I loved it! I'm sooooo happy Nylyan wasn't really dead and it was just a potion to make her heart stop. S

D See, I told you, you had to finish it. ☺

True, you did. S

D Hey . . .

What . . . S

D Are you really busy this weekend?

Here it is. He's going to ask Aggie out.

Um, not too busy. Just hanging around with family. S

D: Go out with me.

S: OK

D: Really???

S: Yes. Why, were you kidding?

D: No, not at all.

D: Cool. Do you want to choose where we go?

S: How about we meet somewhere? How about dinner at Mama Rosa's? Do you know it?

D: Near Beanies, right?

S: Right. How about Saturday at five?

D: Perfect

Perfect, I think.

18

Cici Reno @yogagirl4evr • 47 minutes ago
RAG DOLL POSE - Bend over, allowing your hands to hang like a rag doll's. Clasp your elbows with your hands. Helps to let go of tension and worries.

"**B**egin to move into tree pose," Mom says. "Go ahead and slowly move your right foot up your left inner thigh until you find a comfortable spot. In ancient India, yogis were known to stand on the banks of the Ganges River for days like this, chanting and meditating. They say that your ability to easily hold this posture reflects your emotional state."

I move into tree and I'm feeling wobbly. Great, I think. My emotional state is really top notch today.

"Keep your hands in prayer," Mom continues, "and when you are ready, open your tree."

I push my hands up into the air and fall to my left. Peg gives me a surprised side glance. I never lose my balance like this. I'm too distracted. My mind is supposed to be empty of all thoughts, and I should be concentrating on my breathing but I'm just too nervous. Aggie is meeting Drew in one hour. I thought yoga would calm me down, but it's not working today. Thankfully class is about over.

"You okay, honey?" Mom asks after the rest of the class has left.

"Just having an off day, you know?" I tell her. "I'm going to meet Aggie at Beanies in a few minutes if that's okay." It's a small white lie, but I don't want to get a lecture about ruining dinner. It's not like I'm going to be eating anyway.

"That's fine. Come back when you're done, and I'll take you home. Tell Aggie I can give her a ride if she needs. And Cici, lay off the caffeine, okay? You're awfully jumpy today. Try a fruit smoothie—maybe something with banana."

"I will," I say, and dart out the door. I want to get to Mama Rosa's before Aggie and set things up.

I race over, not bothering to change out of my yoga clothes. Drew isn't going to see me anyway. Not if I can help it.

I scan the restaurant and it's fairly empty. There's a man reading a newspaper in the corner while eating chicken parmesan, and a woman talking loudly on her cell phone while her slice of veggie pizza gets cold. Two people are working, a guy and Mary, this nice lady who always gives Aggie and me a free garlic knot with our pizza. I make a beeline for Mary. She's busily wiping down the counter.

"Hi, Mary, I need a favor," I say.

"Sure, hon, what can I do for you?"

"Let me hide behind the counter."

Mary stops wiping. "What? Who are you hiding from?"

"I can't exactly give you all the details but basically Aggie will be here in a minute, and she's meeting a guy, and she needs me to feed her lines."

Mary's eyebrows shoot up. "Well, that sounds interesting. Why can't she just talk for herself?"

"It's a long story, Mary. I really need this favor. Please?"

"Sorry, sweetie, I can't have customers back behind the counter. I'll get in trouble."

I frown and look around the restaurant. Aside from the long counter separating the customers from the kitchen, there are five small round tables positioned in front of a large glass window. There's a red- and green-lit *pizza* sign hanging in the center of one of the windows, and a few smaller tables outside in front of the restaurant, for those who want to enjoy the weather. The tables inside are covered in red-and-white checkered tablecloths, with matching centerpieces of flickering red-glass battery-operated candles, and single red roses in small bud vases. Somewhere a speaker is piping in background Italian music, and the scent of garlic lingers in the air. There's a tall cooler full of pop on the left side of the restaurant, and that's it, leaving me not many options for a hiding place.

What am I going to do?

"Tell you what," Mary says, coming out from behind the

counter, "why don't you have Aggie sit back here at this table, near the restroom. I have a huge stock of cups in the hallway that I need to unpack today. We can stack the boxes, and you can crouch behind them and hear everything. No one will ever know you're back here."

I look at the boxes. "That could work," I say. "Okay, I'll give it a try. Thanks, Mary." I throw my arms around her for a quick hug.

She laughs. "No problem, hon. I hope this boy's worth all the fuss."

"He is," I assure her.

I look up and see Aggie push through the door into the restaurant. "Ag!" I call, bouncing in place. I wave her over. "Here, sit here." I point to the table. "Mary helped me. It's the perfect spot, since I can hide back here behind the cups."

"Oh, Cici, I'm totally freaking out right now." Aggie slips her light jacket from her shoulders and shakes out her hair. She curled it again for her date. It looks so pretty, I want to pull on one of the curls. She's wearing a fitted striped shirt today, something she hasn't been doing much of since her early onset of boobage.

"I know, me too," I tell her. "Though you're doing all the work. I'll be right here though, listening to everything."

"Right."

"Remember, safe topics: books, movies, and hockey. Try not to stray. And remember, we want him to feel that you like him."

"I know. Remind me what you told me to say about that book, *The Last Token*?" she asks.

"Tell him you're on book four of *The Last Token*. Ask him if Doryan and Nylyan are going to get married and say that you just can't picture them together."

Aggie takes a deep breath. "Okay. *Last Token*, Doryan, Nylyan. How am I going to remember all of this?"

"I'm here, Ag. You can do it." I slip behind the boxes and we wait for Drew to arrive. I peek at Aggie, and she looks so pretty sitting there with the light from the fake candle illuminating her face. Even though we're just at Mama Rosa's, where we've probably eaten a hundred slices of pizza in our lifetime, it still looks like she's about to have the perfect romantic dinner with the boy of my, I mean her, dreams.

Sigh.

Minutes later, I hear Drew walk through the door and greet Aggie. I catch my breath.

"Hey, Drew," she says cautiously.

He slides into the chair opposite her. "Have you been here long? Sorry if I kept you waiting," he adds.

"No, it's fine. I mean, waiting is fine," Aggie says. She knocks over the bud vase and water spills on the table. "Shoot."

"I got it." Drew goes to the counter and grabs a small stack of napkins. He returns to the table, mops up the mess, and sets the vase back up right with the flower in it. "No foul," he says with a smile.

I peek around the boxes to see Aggie shoot a glance in my direction. I point for her to pay attention to Drew.

"So, do you know what you want to eat?" he asks.

Aggie stares at the paper menu on the table like she's never seen it before. "Um, maybe just a slice of pepperoni?"

"Sounds good. I'll get that too. Be right back." Drew makes his way to the counter to place their order.

"Cici!" Aggie hisses as soon as he's out of earshot. "I'm screwing up!"

"No, you're not. You're doing great," I tell her. "He didn't even care. He probably thinks you're even cuter being all clumsy. Remember, talk about the book."

"Sorry about before," Aggie says. Drew must be back.

"Someone will bring the food out to us in a few minutes. I forgot to ask you what you drink and got us a couple of sodas. Is that okay? I can go back and get you something else," he says, setting the drinks down on the table.

Wow, Drew sounds a little nervous too.

"No, soda is fine. I like soda."

I'm straining to hear, but no one is talking. What's going on? Why isn't Aggie making conversation? I pull out my phone and text her, "TALK TO HIM!"

I hear Aggie's phone buzz, and a moment later she texts back, "I don't know what to say!"

I quickly write back. "Try a compliment?" I peer around the boxes and see Drew looking out the window, bored, while Aggie is texting me on her phone. Agh, we're being rude. "Sorry, no more texts. Put your phone away," I send in a final text.

Aggie puts her phone away and gets to lining up the parmesan and salt and pepper shakers on the table in size order.

"So . . . " Drew says.

"So . . . " Aggie repeats. "I really like your shirt. The color's nice. It makes your eyes really, really blue."

Hey, that wasn't bad. Maybe she'll be able to do this after all.

"Thanks. Yours is, uh, nice too," he says.

Aggie giggles. "I don't know why this is so awkward. We talk all the time."

Drew lets out a sigh of relief. "I know, what's with that? We talk so much online and then, when we're face-to-face, it's just like you said. Awkward."

"Maybe we should bring laptops next time and just type to each other," Aggie says.

Wow! She's doing fantastic. Go Aggie!

"Or we can just keep talking until the awkwardness goes away. I'm already feeling more relaxed."

"Me too," Aggie says.

Mary approaches their table and sets down two slices of pepperoni pizza and two garlic knots.

I can hear the two of them start to eat. "Mmm, this is good," she says.

"It is pretty good," he agrees.

They're both silently chewing and Aggie fidgets and looks around the restaurant like she hasn't been here five hundred times before. I rip a flier for guitar lessons off the community bulletin board in the hallway and with the dangling pen write, *Last Token* on the back. I hold it up. Aggie sees it and gives a slight nod.

"So, I wanted to talk to you about *The Last Token*," Aggie says to Drew. "Are Doorman and Nylyan really going to get married?"

"Doryan?"

"What did I say?" Aggie asks.

"Doorman," he says.

"Oh wow, maybe I am still nervous," Aggie says, trying to laugh it off.

I peek through the boxes and can just make out Aggie's hand fidgeting on the parmesan container. Drew reaches out and covers her hand with his.

"Relax," he says. "It's cool. Things are going well."

"Yeah," she squeaks.

Uh-oh. That hand squeeze might send her over the edge.

"So, book four, you know I'm not going to tell you what happens. You have to wait and find out. And no putting the book in time out again," he kids.

Aggie tries to laugh. "Okay, I won't. I guess. Hey, I got something in my eye. I'm going to run to the restroom and check it out."

"Okay," he replies.

Aggie whooshes around the corner, grabbing my arm, and drags me into the restroom. "Time out? You have a time out for books? Is that some smart thing you readers do? Why did you have to tell him I read, anyway? Now he's going to expect me to know stuff about books."

"You do know stuff about books, relax. It's not a big deal. I can loan you the books to read."

"Ugh," she moans, rubbing her temples with her hands. "I have to read enough in school. I'm not going to do it in my free time too."

"Don't even worry about that," I tell her. "Switch the topic. Get him to talk about hockey. That'll take some of the pressure off you."

"All right. We'll talk about hockey." She checks her reflection in the mirror, takes a deep breath, and pushes through the restroom door.

I follow her out and crouch behind the boxes again, getting in position.

"All better, sorry about that," I hear her tell Drew. "Hmm, this pizza really is good. Do you find playing hockey makes you feel like you're starving all the time? I'm always hungry lately from volleyball."

"Totally. There are times I come home from practice and feel like I could eat an entire buffalo."

"That'd be something to see," she jokes.

There. Aggie's loosening up.

"You should come to more of my games," Drew says.

"Sure, I'd really like that," Aggie says.

"You would?" Drew says, sounding a bit surprised.

"Yeah, I like you."

Whoa! Did Aggie really just say that? Why is she suddenly being so forward? We're not forward. We're coy and cute. Sarcastic and silly. Ugh. I smack the box of cups without thinking. The top two boxes go toppling over and fall out into the dining room area, right in front of a waiter carrying a tray of cannolis. The cannolis go flying through the air, and I cover my mouth with both of my hands. Just as Drew is about to take in another mouthful of pizza, he's slapped upside the head with a giant cannoli.

Aggie's mouth drops open in shock.

"What was that?" Drew says, turning his attention toward the waiter, and I crouch as low to the ground as I can behind the remaining boxes.

Aw, man.

"Looks like flying cannoli," Aggie says, giggling. She reaches over and scoops some filling that got on Drew's cheek and tastes it. "Mmm, it's good too."

Drew grins at her, and the waiter rushes over, apologizing profusely as he tries to clean up the mess. Drew tells him it's okay, but he offers to comp their meal and bring them fresh, intact cannolis. On a plate.

Aggie and Drew talk for another twenty minutes or so and it feels like eternity. Finally his mom comes to pick him up.

"I don't want to leave you here alone," he says. "Want me to run out and ask my mom to wait awhile?"

"Oh no," she says. "You go on ahead. I'm actually going to run down the sidewalk to Peony Lane. You know, Cici's mom's studio? I told Cici I'd meet her there."

"Okay," he says, standing. Aggie stands too. "Dinner was fun. I had a nice time hanging out with you," he tells her.

I glimpse around the boxes. Neither one of them is looking down, so they shouldn't see me.

"Same here," Aggie says. She suddenly throws both arms around Drew's neck and gives him a tight squeeze. Drew looks startled at first but then hugs her back.

What the heck, Aggie? What's come over her? I didn't say maul him. Drew is smiling now and he says good-bye and heads for the door. I'm sitting on the ground trying to calm down. I feel like my blood pressure is going crazy. I knew this was coming, that eventually Aggie and Drew would work everything out and officially be together. But she didn't need to go getting all grabby with my . . .

My *what*? He's not technically anything to me. Though it feels like he is.

I need to calm down.

Aggie waits for a pause and then rushes around the stack of boxes to me. "Well?" she says with a huge smile. "That went great, right?"

I try to force a smile. "Great."

19

Cici Reno @yogagirl4evr • 17 minutes ago
SEATED TWIST POSE - Sit cross-legged, left hand on right thigh, twist. Repeat on other side. Helps you breathe when life gets all twisted.

"**T**wo yoga classes in one day?" Claire says when I walk into the room.

"It's been a rough one," I tell her. I toss my towel on the floor and roll out my mat. I take a seat and begin stretching. "You're still here. Are you taking another class?"

"Oh no. I just got caught up chatting and never left. Your mom's back in her office, I think. Bonnie's teaching this class."

"Yeah, I know." I'm actually glad. I don't want Mom asking me what's wrong again.

"Well, if you ever need to talk, I'm around," Claire says.

I smile. Maybe I should talk to Claire about my problems. It's not *that* long ago that she was in middle school, and it's not like she'd ever tell Aggie or anyone else I know. Plus, it's not like I can talk to other kids at school. They always think I'm the one with the answers, not with the problems. I pull my legs into lotus pose.

"Claire, do you ever get jealous? Or, like, did you ever get jealous of other girls in school?"

Claire plops down on the floor next to my mat. "Of course! Jealousy is practically required in school. In fact, I still get jealous, even now. In school you are just forced to spend a lot of time with other people, so it's only natural to get jealous from time to time. You can't avoid it. It's like when people only show photos of their great vacations. You can't help but wish that was your life."

"Yeah." I nod. I get what she's saying. It's sorta the same online, seeing what everyone else is doing and all. But it's different when the person you're jealous of is right in front of you, not behind a screen. How do you hide your jealousy then? "I'll just tell you what's going on. It's basically the guy I really, really like likes my best friend. And it's hard seeing that."

"Oh," Claire says. She twists her lips and looks deep in thought. "Well, you're right about that. That's rough. And how does Aggie feel about him?"

"She likes him too. Actually, she liked him first. But I know him better. We talk more. We'd make a better couple, but she has dibs."

"Hmm. All I can tell you is that good friends, best friends, are hard to come by, and there will be many boys in your lifetime. Sisters before misters, you know?"

Sure. But this mister is different.

Bonnie walks in. Class is about to start.

"I'm not sure if I've helped you with your problem at all," Claire says, slowly getting to her feet.

"I'll think about what you said. It helps to talk to someone who's not involved."

"Just remember, everything gets better with time. Even if a situation seems horrible today, tomorrow will be a bit better." Claire gives me a hug, tucks her mat under her arm, and heads for the door.

• • •

There should be a state law that school cannot begin until noon on Mondays. An eight AM bell is way unfair.

"Cici!" I hear Aggie scream after I've walked about ten steps into school. I look around trying to locate her. She pushes through a mob of sixth graders and is in front of me a moment later. "I made the volleyball team!" she yells, hopping up and down.

"Congratulations!" I shriek and join her in the hopping. "I knew you would! You were the best one at tryouts. I'm so happy for you!" And I really am. I thought about it a lot last night, and Claire was right. Aggie's my best friend and you don't come by best friends easily. I said I was going to help her get Drew and I did, so everything is right. I just need to squash my feelings and be happy for them. They do look perfect together.

"I can't believe it," she continues. "I thought I had a good chance after tryouts. I mean, it felt good, you know? But wow, I really made it. I have to call my mom. Our first practice is after school today."

"Hey, Aggie," a male voice says. We look up and see Drew, my brother Luke, and their friend Austin. Luke is looking around like he wants to be absolutely anywhere else in the world right now besides standing in a hallway with his sister.

"Drew, hi! I made the team!" Aggie squeals, hopping up and down again.

"Wow, congrats!" he says. He leans over and gives her a big hug.

She hugs him back, an enormous grin on her face.

My stomach lurches. I can't take my eyes off her face. She says something else, and he responds, but I'm not really listening. Seeing them together just . . . hurts. Drew and the guys walk off, probably on their way to the eighth grade hallway, and I'm still staring at Aggie.

She gives me a puzzled look. "You okay, Cici?"

I speak slowly, thinking about how I want to say this. "I'm fine. You two just . . . really look like a couple now."

"All thanks to you!" she says. "We probably would have never said two words to each other if it weren't for you."

I'm trying hard to smile like everything is fine, but the pain is welling up so much inside that I have to get out of here, away from Aggie, before I say the wrong thing.

"Sure. I'm always here for you. But right now I need to get to class. If I'm late one more time I'll get detention, and . . . " I turn and practically run toward English.

"Cici, got a second?" Tina Smith, another seventh grader, calls out to me, leaning against a row of lockers.

"Later!" I yell. "I'm in a hurry." I can't help anyone else right now. I can't even help myself.

20

 Cici Reno @yogagirl4evr • 21 minutes ago
CAMEL POSE - Kneel, stretch, and reach back,
placing your hands on your feet. Drop your head
back. Helps you to release powerful emotions.

Today was so weird. I was upset and then okay and then upset again. I don't know why this whole situation with Drew keeps getting to me. I keep reminding myself that I created this. It's not like my best friend is stealing my boyfriend. Drew isn't involved with me. But still, it feels like he is.

Aggie asked me at lunch what was wrong and I told her "Nothing," of course, but she could sense it. And when Madison and Alexa came to our lunch table all giggly and asking Aggie if it was true she was dating an eighth grader, I felt like I was punched in the gut. Aggie glanced at me and then told the girls she wasn't sure if they were labeling their relationship.

Labeling *THEIR* relationship.

CHAPTER TWENTY

That night after I finish dinner and my homework I go to my room and check my messages, though I don't expect there to be anything, now that I'm not needed anymore. Aggie and Drew are together, and I'm alone.

I'm shocked to see a message waiting for me from Drew. I should probably call Aggie and tell her; let her handle it. But I can't resist. I open the message.

> **D**   Are you mad at me?

Mad at him? Why would he think Aggie would be mad at him? She was just hanging all over him at school.

I'm sure she'd want me to say no. It wouldn't hurt to respond this one time.

> No, why?   **S**

There's no response for a full minute. How long does it take him to type? Finally a message pops up.

> **D**   You blew me off today, after school.

What? No way. Aggie wouldn't do that. And she didn't tell me anything about seeing Drew after school. How did she blow him off? I don't know how to respond.

> I did?   **S**

> **D**   Yeah. When I stopped in at your first volleyball practice to wish you luck.

Oh yikes. She must have blown him off then. I'll just fix this for her. She'd want me to.

> I'm sorry. I was really nervous.   **S**

> **D** You didn't look nervous.

> Well, you know what they say about looks being deceiving. **S**

Boy, ain't that the truth.

> **D** So you're not mad?

> Uh-uh. **S**

> **D** Got time to chat?

I think about this. I desperately want to talk to Drew. I love talking to him. We have a special bond.

> Yep. **S**

> **D** ☺

> Hey, guess what I just got? **S**

> **D** Book five of The Last Token?

> No, but good guess. I have that on hold at the library. I got a light up Minecraft torch! It's so cool. **S**

> **D** Oh wow, where'd you get it?

> My mom got it online somewhere. It's hanging over my bed now. **S**

> **D** Nice!

I settle back in my chair, ready for a long chat with Drew.

• • •

At school the next day, I invite Aggie to take a yoga class with me when she's done with practice. I think we both could use it. We're both feeling stress from our current situation, and yoga should help at least a little with that. Before school, I had filled Aggie in about my chat with Drew last night. I didn't want her to think I was doing something sneaky. And I was curious why Drew had thought she blew him off. She said she didn't exactly mean to, but she didn't want her new volleyball friends to think they were together. Which is odd.

I'm walking out to my mom's car in the parking lot when I see my friend Grace from English in the pickup line, looking teary.

"What's wrong, Grace?" I say when I approach her.

She looks startled. "Just a bad day."

"Do you want to talk?" I ask.

Grace looks around before she responds. "Sophie and I got into a fight in gym class. A really stupid one. I tried to apologize, but she's mad at me now and wouldn't say anything. Just stormed off."

I shake my head. Fights with your best friend are no fun, I know it. I can totally sympathize. Aggie and I aren't in a fight but our friendship is feeling some obvious strain. "She probably just needed to blow off a little steam," I tell Grace. "Give her some breathing space and see how things are tomorrow. She can't stay mad for long."

"I don't know about that," Grace says, a worry line creasing her forehead.

"I'm telling you, things will look different in the morning.

If she still won't talk to you when you see her before school, then try to apologize again. I know how close you and Sophie are. I don't think she'll be able to stay mad at you."

"I hope you're right." Her chin quivers.

"You need to relax. Come to yoga with Aggie and me tonight. We're taking a five PM class at my mom's studio. You'll feel much better, I bet. And if that doesn't work, we'll get something chocolaty at Beanies."

Grace considers this. "Okay, I'll ask my mom to drop me off."

"Great," I say. Not only will this help Grace's mood, but having her there will be a good buffer for Aggie and me. Things are still a little weird between us.

• • •

I'm sitting in the lobby at Peony Lane doing my homework. It's about four o'clock, so I have another hour before Grace and Aggie show up for class. I'm checking my assignment notebook again when Luke and Drew walk in.

"Hang out with Cici for a minute while I run in back and talk to my mom," Luke tells Drew.

Drew nods and sits down right next to me on the sofa. "Hey, Cici. What are you working on, math?"

"Yeah, algebra," I say. "Math is dependable. There's always a right or wrong answer. No guessing or trying to interpret what something means."

"Like in literature?" he asks.

"Exactly," I reply. Or like in relationships. Boys. You.

Aggie. You know, everything. Not that I say this. "So have things gotten better with you and Aggie since last we talked?"

He sighs heavily. "Well, I guess. I mean, our whole relationship is really strange. She's hot, then cold, then hot, then cold. Something is off but I can't figure it out."

"What do you mean?" I ask, tentatively.

Drew smirks. "You're going to think I'm such a whiner. And I shouldn't complain. I don't know what I'm expecting really."

"Tell me," I urge.

"Okay, so like, remember when I was telling you Aggie's so cool when we're chatting online and then acts like she hates me in person?"

"Right, but then you guys went on a date . . . " I lead. He gives me a surprised look. "Oh, you know, best friends talk," I say. "I heard the date went great."

"It did . . . I guess," he says. "No, I mean, ugh. I can't believe I'm telling you this stuff. Promise me you won't say anything. I could just be misinterpreting things."

I motion crossing my heart.

"When we're together it's like we don't quite click. It feels forced. Not natural, you know?"

"That's strange," I say.

"I know," he says. "When we're chatting online she talks so freely and we have a lot of common interests. Then when we're together she's reserved or holding back, and it feels off. And she doesn't talk about the same stuff either. Like, she never talks about volleyball online, but in person she talks about it constantly. I told you it's crazy. Just a random feeling I get. Don't tell her I said anything, okay?"

"I won't," I reassure him. How bad is it that I feel relief to hear him say these things?

"I don't know why I'm even so invested. It's like I keep waiting for her to be the girl I talk to online, and she just isn't. The Aggie I talk to every night is perfect for me."

I smile.

"Ahhhh, I'm such a sap. You're too easy to tell all of this stuff to, Cici. Promise me you won't let it get around what a loser I am. Don't tell your brother either; he already thinks I'm being a moron. He doesn't get why I'm trying so hard with Aggie. He said all he sees when he looks at her is the girl who picked her nose all through second grade and carried around a collection of plastic doll heads everywhere she went."

"Oh yeah," I say. "She did have a great doll head collection. And Luke should talk. I could tell you disgusting stories about him all afternoon."

"I bet," Drew says.

"All right, we're out of here," Luke says, walking back into the lobby.

"Cool," Drew says, standing up. He bends toward me and gives my shoulder a quick squeeze. "Thanks for the talk," he whispers.

I feel my cheeks blush at his touch. "No problem," I reply.

21

Cici Reno @yogagirl4evr • 36 minutes ago
ONE-LEGGED DOWNWARD DOG POSE - From
Downward Dog, stretch out one leg over and
behind. Helps you see a person's beauty from the
inside out.

Mom rarely lets me work the front desk at Peony
Lane, but I sure love it when she does. You can
see everything from up here. All the people walking back
and forth in front of the studio, going shopping with their
moms, or on dates with cute boys. There's so much living
going on just past this window and I love watching it all. Not
that there isn't a bunch of living going on inside of course.
People coming out of yoga are always very chill and Zen.
I've heard more than one client refer to it as life-altering.
There's definitely some important stuff happening in here. I
once asked Mom what she would be if she hadn't become a
yogini and opened her own studio. She said, "Crabby."

Yoga with Aggie and Grace ended up being fun
yesterday evening. Grace looked ten times cheerier when

she left, and Aggie and I goofed around like everything was completely fine. Drew's name didn't come up even once and I'm glad of that. When we're not talking about him everything feels normal between us. I tried to get the girls to do some partner yoga with me and get into a Triple Down Dog with Grace doing a downward dog on her mat, Aggie doing a downward dog with her feet on Grace's back, and me doing a downward dog with my feet on Aggie's back. We mostly just kept giggling and falling over though. We'll have to practice more if we want to pull that one off.

"Your mom's got you working, eh?" Peg asks as she comes through the door, mat tucked under her arm; she's wearing a sleeveless white shirt with "I woke up like this" written in black sequins.

"Yep," I reply. "Bonnie and Jackson are out, and Wendy's teaching a hot yoga class at the same time as Mom's class tonight, so I get to run the desk."

"Well, you are just cute as a bug sitting back there, looking so grown-up," Peg adds.

And this is the reason why Mom doesn't like me running the front desk. She thinks it looks unprofessional for clients coming in to see a kid working. But I'm practically thirteen and besides, no one cares!

"Hey girls," Claire says, walking into the studio.

Peg high-fives Claire, then bends to start stretching. "So what's the update with Aggie? Things settle down?"

I smile. "Yeah. She's going to be fine. Really I'd say things are almost back to normal."

"And the boy?" Claire asks.

The boy. Hmm. There's still that. I don't know what to do to fix the situation with Drew. I would kind of like the whole thing to just go away. For him to not like Aggie and Aggie to not like him, and for them to never speak or date or even be aware of each other's existence. But without losing our nightly chats that I love so much. I'd hate to lose that. If only Drew could like me back the way that I like him.

"Um," I say to Claire, "I'm just sort of stepping aside for now. Our friendship is the most important thing, and I don't want to wreck that."

"That's so good to hear," Peg chimes in. "You're restoring my faith in humanity."

"Thanks," I say.

"Well, I better get into class now before I get stuck in the back with a bunch of rear ends in my face," Peg says.

I giggle as Peg and Claire head into their class. Maybe things are finally turning around.

• • •

After Mom and I get home and we all have dinner, I go to my room to do my homework. And check my messages of course. There isn't anything from Drew waiting for me, which is kind of surprising. I've gotten used to him at least sending me a note each night, even if he can't chat.

I get a craving for some ice cream and head out to the kitchen to see what we have in the freezer. I come to an abrupt stop when I see Drew sitting at my kitchen counter, his laptop open in front of him and Luke's laptop sitting opposite his. But no Luke. I briefly panic as I look down at my outfit. Darn it, I'm wearing my old Care Bears pajama pants and a faded "Girls Rock" T-shirt, and here's Drew looking amazing in a black hoodie. Great.

"Drew," I say, "what are you doing here?"

"Hey, Cici," Drew says, looking up from his laptop. "Nice pants."

Ugh. "Thanks," I say.

"I'm sleeping over tonight. We have an early morning hockey practice, and my mom can't drive me, so your mom suggested I sleep over and she's going to take us," he says.

Sleeping over? Drew Lancaster is spending the entire night in my house? Oh my gosh, oh my gosh, oh my gosh.

"No one told me," I say. "I mean, not that anyone has to tell me, it's just, I didn't know. Want some ice cream?"

"Sure," Drew says.

I busy myself pulling out the ice cream, chocolate syrup, whipped cream, and some bowls. "Where's my brother, anyway?" I ask.

"Luke went to take a shower," Drew says.

So we're completely alone. Yikes. "Want to put your own toppings on?" I ask, pushing a bowl of ice cream toward him.

"Yeah, thanks," he says. "Hey, maybe you can help me with something," he adds.

"Sure," I say. I work on scooping ice cream into a bowl.

"I need you to help me break up with Aggie."

"What?" I practically screech, my scoop-holding hand flicking right, sending a ball of ice cream across the room and landing in the fruit bowl on the counter. I look at the blob of vanilla. "Oops." I rip some paper towels off the roll and work on cleaning up the mess. "I mean, why would you want to break up with Aggie?"

Drew takes a seat at his laptop, ice cream in hand. "I was going to send her a message tonight and I've just been sitting here trying to think of how to say it. I'm not even sure she would care, to tell you the truth."

"What do you mean? Of course she cares," I insist.

Drew shakes his head. "Nah. She totally blew me off at school again today."

"Are you sure?" I ask. I toss out the paper towels and take a seat next to Drew. "I mean, maybe you misread her?"

Drew laughs. "Oh, I didn't misread her. I was heading out of school and Aggie was walking with some girl toward the gym for her volleyball practice. I said something like, 'talk to you tonight,' and she just stared at me and then went back to talking to her friend. It was totally embarrassing."

"Really?" I say. "That's so bizarre. It doesn't sound like Aggie at all. I wonder if something is going on. Did she look sick or anything?"

"No. Maybe sick of me," he jokes.

"Oh, Drew, I'm sure that's not it. Aggie only talks about you really positively, I promise."

He shrugs and stares at the cursor flashing in his open message to SeraFrosted. I have to think of a way to stop him. If he stops talking to Aggie, he stops talking to me.

"Tell you what," I say. "Don't do anything rash. Don't break up with her but just don't write her either. Make her come to you. Let her explain why she's acting so weird. In the meantime, I'll have a talk with her."

"No," Drew says. "Don't do that; I'm going to look so lame."

"No, you won't," I insist. "I'm not going to tell her you put me up to it or anything. Let me just see where her head is at. If she's not really into you, I'll let you know, and then you can end things gracefully, without looking bad, you know?"

"Really? You want to help me even though she's your best friend?" he asks.

"She's still my best friend. I'm not doing anything shady. I don't want to see either of you hurt."

Drew smiles. "Okay. Thanks."

"Sure," I say, returning his smile.

"Hey, you want to see a picture I'm working on?" he asks.

"You draw?" I ask, surprised. Wow, something I didn't already know about Drew.

"Yeah." He opens a picture of a tough-looking half-man, half-tree character.

The picture is really good, like professionally good.

"Whoa, you drew this?" I'm totally impressed. "That is so awesome!"

Drew looks pleased. "Yeah, it's not finished yet though. I like to draw a lot of stuff. I don't really show people usually."

"You should. It's really, really good," I tell him.

"Thanks," he says. Just then Luke walks into the kitchen, hair still damp from his shower. Out of the corner of my eye I notice Drew quickly close the picture on his laptop.

"Dessert?" Luke asks.

"Yep, help yourself," I tell him, pushing the half gallon of ice cream his way. I finish putting the toppings on my own bowl and turn to leave the kitchen.

Drew gives me a quick wink as I go.

22

Cici Reno @yogagirl4evr • 21 minutes ago
FISH POSE - Lie back, rest on your elbows, extend
your legs. Arch back so the crown of your head
touches the floor. Helps you to forgive.

"**G**ot everything you need, hon? Do you need money?
You girls aren't going anywhere, right?" Mom asks as
she pulls the minivan into Aggie's driveway on Saturday night.

"Yes, always, and I don't think so," I say.

"Ha ha. Here, take some cash with you," Mom says,
reaching into her purse. "Just in case you go out to a movie
or something."

"Ooh, thanks, Mom!" I let myself out of the car, pulling
my backpack and sleeping bag with me, and head up to
Aggie's house.

Before I even ring the doorbell Aggie whips open the
door. "Hey!" she says.

On Aggie's side, her little brother, Henry, comes
barreling toward me. He leaps and I drop my stuff on the

ground, ready to catch him. "Hold me!" he yells.

"Gotcha!" I say, laughing. "You know, one of these days you're going to catch me off guard, and I'll miss, right?"

I set my stuff on the floor in their foyer and let Henry lead me to their living room floor to play. Ten minutes later, Aggie flips on *Mickey Mouse Clubhouse*, and Henry has lost all interest in me. He's standing in front of the television mimicking Goofy's dance moves.

Aggie motions for me to follow her to her room, and we sneak out of the living room.

We plop onto Aggie's bed and she pulls open a small crate of nail polish. "Pick a color," she says.

"Hmm, mint green," I say, taking the bottle.

"I'm going with school colors, red and blue," she tells me and we set to work on painting our nails. "By the way, my mom wanted me to ask if you're sure your mom can give me a ride to the fall dance on Friday."

"Of course we can," I say. "Aak! I got paint all over my pinky finger." Aggie hands me a tissue to wipe with. "In fact, can you just come home from school with us? Then we can get ready together, maybe do a facial or something beforehand so we're extra glowy."

"That sounds fun. I'll ask my mom," Aggie says. "So, guess what? My first volleyball game is this Wednesday after school, and I'm starting!"

"That's so cool, Aggie! See, I said you were the best one on the team," I tell her.

"I'm so excited," she says. "And my mom and Carlos and Henry are all going to come watch."

"Oh, Henry is going to go completely ape when he sees you out there. We have to make him a little sign with your name and number to wave around like a banner. And your mom is cool with the whole volleyball thing now, huh?"

"Yeah," Aggie says. "I think when she realized it was something I was good at and that didn't really take away from home or school or anything, she relaxed about it. She's excited for me. She even came to one of the practices and took pictures of me playing. I sent them to my dad and stepmom too. They said they wished they could come to a game."

"Your mom should take a video you can send them," I say. "And you know I'll be there, cheering you on."

"Oh good, you can make it?" she asks.

"Of course. I may even make a banner to match Henry's," I kid.

I'm blowing on my fingernails when an idea comes to me. "Hey, Aggie, Drew said something about going to the volleyball game too. Do you care if he goes? I mean, he can sit with me if you want."

She shrugs. "No, why would I care? Anyone can go to the volleyball games. I just hope he doesn't expect me to talk to him during the game. I need to concentrate on what I'm doing."

Huh? Where's this attitude coming from? "I'm sure he won't expect you to," I tell her.

Aggie stops working on her nails and looks at me. "Why would he sit with you though?"

Good question. "Um, we've sort of been becoming . . . friends."

"Really? When did this start?"

"It's not a big deal or anything. We've just been talking, and I don't mean online as you. He and I have been talking some in person lately. Most of the time we're actually talking about you, but still. We're sorta friends, I guess."

"What do you mean you're talking about me? What are you saying about me?" she asks.

Aggie is sounding slightly angry with me, and I'm not sure why. "Just convincing him that you don't hate him," I say. "He's getting mixed signals because we talk one way online and then when he sees you in person, well, you had that great date, but I guess you sort of blow him off sometimes. Which is no big deal, really. Don't worry about it. I've been covering for all that."

"Oh yeah. So he noticed that, huh?" Aggie says. She looks down and away.

"So you *are* blowing him off?" I ask, shocked. "Why?! He said it's happened a couple of times, but I made excuses for you!"

She shrugs, still avoiding making eye contact with me. "I don't think I like him the way I thought I did. I guess I thought I liked him because it was fun to have a crush on someone when we went to hockey games, you know, to cheer for someone and be silly. And it seems like all our friends have crushes on somebody, so it was the thing to do. But now that he's like, in my world, talking to me at school, wanting to meet places, and be all couple-y, I just don't have any real feelings for him. I'm not ready for the whole boyfriend thing, I think. And he's not all that interesting, to tell you the truth," she adds.

I gasp. "Are you kidding me? Drew's smart and kind and funny, no, make that hysterical. He tells the best stories ever and he's so creative. Did you know he draws? He's like the definition of interesting," I say, abruptly stopping. Maybe I went on a little too much. Aggie's just staring at me with wide eyes.

"Cici," she starts, "do *you* like Drew?"

And there it is, laying out smack dab in the middle of us. The truth.

"No, no. I mean, well, I don't know." I pause and swallow hard. "Would you be upset if I did? Like him?"

Aggie thinks about this, and I twist my ring around and around my finger. "I feel like it should upset me," she finally says. "If I had feelings for him, that is. But no, I don't think it bothers me. If you really like him, you should go after him."

"Oh, I couldn't do that. He'd never like me that way. I'm not his type at all. You're his type. I'd have to grow on him." I shrug. "Maybe if we keep talking online for a while I can eventually tell him. Kinda ease into it."

"But he thinks SeraFrosted is me," Aggie protests.

CHAPTER TWENTY-TWO

"True," I agree. "I'd have to think of a way to change that."

"Well, think of something sooner than later. I don't want him to keep thinking we're an item. I'm kinda over Drew and the whole dating thing."

Over Drew. Those two words sound insane together. How can anyone be over Drew? I nod. "I'll fix everything."

• • •

I told Aggie I was going to fix everything, but I still don't know how I'm going to manage that. The whole situation goes round and round in my head all the time and I can't figure out a way to make it stop without someone getting hurt. The one thing I know I have to do is reach out to Drew first. Tonight. He's been true to his word and hasn't sent me, SeraFrosted, a single message in two days.

> I've missed you. **S**

I stare at the screen waiting for a message to appear but nothing. He must not be online now. I switch to see what other people are doing tonight. Some are talking about homework, television shows, a lot of boring stuff. Lots of blah, blah, blah. I see a flicker on the corner of the page. It's Drew.

> **D** Hey.

That's it? Just a "Hey?"

> What are you up to tonight? **S**

> **D** Not much. Thinking about watching some TV.

His answers are so stiff. He really is mad at me.

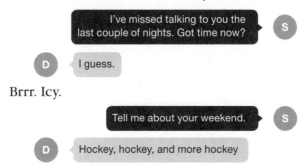

> I've missed talking to you the last couple of nights. Got time now? **S**

> **D** I guess.

Brrr. Icy.

> Tell me about your weekend. **S**

> **D** Hockey, hockey, and more hockey

This whole situation we're in is absurd. Drew wants to break up with Aggie, Aggie wants to break up with Drew, and here I am trying to keep some kind of relationship going between them online, because I can't let it go.

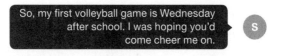

> So, my first volleyball game is Wednesday after school. I was hoping you'd come cheer me on. **S**

I wait for a response. He must be thinking, because it's taking a moment.

> **D** Really? You want me there?

> Yes! My family is all coming too. And Cici of course. You can sit with her if you want. **S**

> OK I'll be there.

> **D** Tell me about your weekend.

I let out a big sigh. Good. He's going to forgive me. Now maybe we can both relax and just chat.

23

Cici Reno @yogagirl4evr • 21 minutes ago
DEAD BUG POSE - Lie on your back, bend your
knees, grab the outside of each foot. Helps you
relieve tension when you're stressed.

"**W**hose bright idea were these giant pom-poms?"
I ask Aggie. We're in the girls' locker room, and
she's sitting in front of me on a bench while I try to wrestle
this massive red and blue pom-pom onto her ponytail.

"One of the moms made them," Aggie says. "She thought
it would look cute if we were all matching for the first game."

"It's definitely cute, just looks a little heavy to hold up,"
I tell her.

"It's not. But the ponytail is starting to give me a headache."

I work on loosening up her ponytail to give her
some relief. "There, you're perfect. Just don't let anyone
accidentally try to spike it off your head thinking it's the
volleyball."

Aggie laughs. "Ah, I'm so nervous!"

"Don't be, you'll be great," I say.

Aggie's volleyball coach bellows into the locker room, calling all the girls for warm-up.

"I guess I better go," I say. "Good luck!"

"Thanks," Aggie mouths as she follows the other girls out of the room.

I head into the gym and scan the bleachers. There are a ton of people here. I spot Drew, front and center, just behind where our Wright Middle School team sits when they're on the bench. I gulp. I hope Aggie's not annoyed that he's so close. Drew's standing and waving to me now, and I make my way over to him.

"Hi, Drew," I say, taking the empty spot to his right.

"How's Aggie?" he asks.

"Good," I tell him. "Nervous, but good. And that's with balancing a beach ball on her head like a seal."

"What?" He raises his eyebrows.

I smile. "Just a little hair accessorizing the girls have going on."

The teams come out onto the floor and start warming up. Drew spots Aggie and says, "Oh, I see what you mean. Those are cute."

He would say they were cute. Aggie can make anything look cute. I scan the bleachers to see who else is here, and I spot Aggie's family at the top. Henry is leaning against the wall with his hands in the air, cheering. Aggie sees him and waves. She spots Drew and me and waves and smiles at us.

Drew waves back eagerly. A small fraction of the school band is here and they're slowly clunking through the school song. Everyone seems really excited.

The game begins, and Aggie is serving first. She nails it, but someone on the other side returns it. I don't know much about the game, but they seem to be keeping the ball up in the air and passing it back and forth. Every so often a guy on a ladder at the net blows a whistle and points one way or the other.

Drew has his attention fixed on the game and Aggie. I'm studying her now too. I had no idea they wore such tight little bicycle shorts with their jerseys tucked in for volleyball. Doesn't anyone think that shows a little too much? The other team has on a similar outfit only in gold and green. What's wrong with nice roomy sweatpants?

Drew leans toward me. "She's really good, huh?"

"Yeah, she's great," I say as enthusiastically as I can. "Go Aggie!" I yell out. Hmm. I'm not sure she was doing anything just now, but she'll know I meant well.

Minutes go by and our side gets a point, making the score 3-1. I spot Sophie and Grace sitting together in the bleachers near the gym entrance. They look pretty happy. Awesome, they must have made up. I want to go over and say hi.

"Hey, Drew," I say, "I'm going to run out and get a snack from the concession stand. Want anything?"

He doesn't take his eyes off the game. "Nah, I'm good."

Well, as long as he's good. I stand and make my way

toward the exit, stopping by Sophie and Grace. "Hey, girls!"

"Cici," they say at the same time and then giggle.

Yep, things are definitely back to normal with them.

"Where are you sitting?" Sophie asks.

I point. "Over there, near the team."

"Aggie's really good!" Grace says.

"Yeah, she's great," I agree. "Cheer loudly so she hears you." I wave good-bye and keep making my way out to where the snacks are.

I return to the gym doors five minutes later, box of candy in hand. Before I even start back for my seat I notice Drew isn't there. Aggie's sitting on the bench and Drew's kneeling next to her, talking.

Oh no. I'm frozen. I don't know what to do. It's not like I can charge over there and tell him to stop talking to Aggie. And I had promised her I wouldn't let him bother her during her first game. Ugh! I hope she's not mad. Though, now that I look closer, she doesn't really look mad. She's actually smiling. And talking a lot. Drew tosses his head back, laughing. Maybe Aggie's changed her mind. Maybe she was hasty in saying she wasn't interested in Drew and now she really is. What if they end up together after all?

I'm not so sure I want to share my candy with him anymore.

I stand there at the gymnasium doors until Aggie rotates back into the game and Drew returns to our seats. I know I have to go back and sit down or he'll start to wonder what happened to me. I take a deep breath and make my way back to our seats.

"Hey, I'm back," I say, stating the obvious.

Drew smiles up at me. "Great game, right?"

I glance at the court. "Oh yeah, it's . . . great."

Aggie jumps up and spikes the ball, scoring another point for our side and the stands erupt in cheers. Drew stands up next to me, clapping along with everyone else and yelling for Aggie.

"Awesome!" he says, retaking his seat.

"Totally," I agree.

"Hey, I want to thank you, by the way."

"For what?" I ask him.

"For talking to Aggie for me. I don't know what you said, but everything seems good. Really good. I think we may work out after all," he tells me.

"That's wonderful," I say. And by wonderful I mean in that heart being ripped out of your chest, thrown to the ground, and danced on by a five-hundred-pound sumo wrestler–kind of way.

"Candy?" I pour about half the box into his hand. I figure, the more he's busy chewing on hard caramels, the less I have to hear about how awesome things are with Aggie now.

I look at Aggie on the court and she's giving us a thumbs-up. Drew returns the sign and I sink lower on my seat, hugging my knees.

24

Cici Reno @yogagirl4evr • 25 minutes ago
FROG POSE - Kneel with elbows supporting you,
palms flat. Knees out. Clench your thigh and back
muscles. Helps you relax before dancing.

Mom drops Luke, Aggie, and me off at the fall dance.
She threatened to sign up as one of the chaperones,
but Luke begged her not to. I don't know why he's making
such a big deal about her being there. I bet he doesn't even
dance with anyone. He'll probably sit in the corner with his
friends being goofy and loud.

I'm wearing a silver glittery sweater dress with tights
and my favorite boots that have a good inch and a half heel.
Mom won't let me get real heels yet. She thinks heels are
stupid and doesn't get why women torture themselves in
them. She says if they want their calves to look good, then
they should exercise more. Aggie helped me curl my hair,
and it actually looks really good. I should have asked her to
help me with it long ago.

Aggie looks great tonight too. She's wearing a pink deco tulle dress, and it looks adorable on her. I send out a picture of us at my house before we left with the message:

Cici Reno @yogagirl4evr • 24 minutes ago
About to get our dance on! #AWMS #dance #BFFs #soexcited

In a message after Wednesday night's volleyball game, Drew asked her, AKA me/SeraFrosted, to go to the dance with him, but I said no. I didn't do it meanly or anything. I just reminded him that my mom won't let me date yet and she would consider that technically a date. I told him I was going with my girlfriends and would see him there though.

I talked to Aggie after the volleyball game too, to get the scoop on her and Drew's relationship and if there was one again. I told her I would step aside if she had changed her mind, but she just laughed and said no. She was only being nice to him. Drew is such a nice guy, so I can see that she wouldn't ignore him or anything. I didn't tell her all the stuff he had said about their relationship working out after all. I still have to figure out what to do about that.

Luke wanders away from us to look for his friends, and Aggie and I head straight for the gym. We push through the heavy wooden doors, and the gym looks amazing. The theme is "Starry Night," and there are lines of twinkle lights woven back and forth through the wooden ceiling beams across the entire gym. Suspended from the light strands are various sizes of white and silver stars hanging from different lengths of string. The floor is covered in white and silver balloons, and Aggie and I kick them away as we enter.

"It's so magical!" I say.

"Look! A DJ!" Aggie says, pointing at what looks like a high school boy standing behind a silver cloth–covered table full of equipment and a couple of laptops.

"Ooh, and look over there." I point to a black backdrop covered in stars, with a big round moon hanging from a string in front of it. "I think that's for taking pictures."

"Maybe you can take a picture with Drew," Aggie suggests with a sly grin.

I raise my eyebrows and shrug. While that would be completely wonderful, I don't see it happening. Still, I find myself scanning the whole room, hoping to catch a glimpse of him. I wonder what he's wearing tonight.

"Cici, Aggie!" London calls to us over the music. We turn and see her, Emma, Madison, and Alexa headed our way.

"Let's get a picture together," Emma says.

We make our way over to the backdrop and pose with our arms draped around each other's shoulders, and the mom playing photographer for the evening takes our picture.

After the photo, London becomes super-serious all of a sudden. "You guys, I need your help tonight. You have to warn me if you see Adam with *her*. I just, I can't bear seeing them with their arms all over each other or anything."

"Aw, Lon," I say, "of course we will," and the others nod.

London has been recovering slowly from her heartbreak, and I can imagine it would be devastating to see Adam with Katie. Rumor has it, they're an official couple now.

"Oh my gosh, you guys, look!" Aggie squeals. Our gaze follows to where she's pointing. "It's Mr. Adwell dancing with Ms. Stoll, the librarian!"

It's true. They're both bopping and swinging around, not at all to the beat of the music, but they're smiling so much, I don't think they care.

"They shouldn't have all the fun. Let's go!" Alexa says. She grabs my hand and pulls me toward the dance floor. I grab Aggie, and she grabs London, and so on, and we chain our way to the middle of the dance floor.

We're having so much fun dancing like crazy. We're spinning in circles and laughing and taking turns dipping each other and I'm getting totally sweaty. Thankfully, a slow song comes on, and I motion to Aggie that we should go get something to drink. We head for the gymnasium doors and we're almost out to the hallway, when Aggie suddenly stops. I turn to see what halted her, and I see Drew take her hand in his. He's pulling her toward the dance floor. Aggie looks at me and shrugs like "what can I do?" as she lets him pull her back to the center of the gym.

I can feel my breath catch as I watch him put his hands around her waist and see her rest her hands on his shoulders. They're swaying in time to the music and my heart is beating so hard I can feel it in my ears. That should be me out there with Drew, not Aggie.

He smiles down at her, not taking his eyes off of her for a second, even though I can see Luke and the other boys hooting and laughing off at the side of the gym. Drew couldn't care less though. His attention is 100 percent on Aggie.

My brain is telling me to stop staring at them. To go on, leave the gym, and take a break. Get a drink of water and let the blood drain from my face and visit the other parts of my body. But my legs are saying no, stay here. Torso needs help holding up this heart that's being torn in two.

And then the worst thing imaginable happens. Despite the loud chaotic gym, all the kids dancing, the boys in the corner making a ruckus, despite it all, Drew leans down and kisses Aggie. On the lips.

25

Cici Reno @yogagirl4evr • 5 minutes ago
WOODCHOPPER POSE - Stand in a wide stance. Clasp your hands and raise above your head as if holding an ax. Swing down hard between legs as if chopping wood, yelling HA! on the exhale. Helps you to release anger.

I feel sick.

I turn, stumbling for the door, and run out of the gym, down the hall, and out of the school into the cool night. I bend over at the bike rack, grabbing the metal bar, coughing and spitting, waiting to throw up. My chest is tight, and it's difficult to breathe. I'm feeling dizzy, like I could pass out right on this spot. The air is hitting my arms and the back of my neck, everywhere I was just sweating from dancing, making me cold. And my cheeks. I reach up and touch my cheeks. I'm crying.

I can't believe she kissed him. That he kissed her. My Drew. Aggie and Drew kissed. I can hardly make sense of it. I squat down and try to even out my breath. I need to calm down, but I can't stop crying.

"Cici?" Aggie calls from the school door.

I straighten up, quickly wiping my eyes and cheeks with the back of my hands. I don't want her to see me like this.

"Cici, are you out here?" she says.

Maybe if I don't say anything she won't see me and will go back inside.

"There you are," she says, and I hear her jogging toward me.

"Cici, look at me. Turn around," Aggie urges.

I shake my head no, not sure I can speak yet.

"Hey, are you mad? You're not mad at me, right? That wasn't my fault. I didn't know he was going to kiss me. He just did it. It's not like I kissed him back." She pauses. "If anything, I made a bit of a scene. I sorta pushed him away from me and told him he shouldn't have done that. I left him standing alone on the dance floor."

I turn and face her. Her eyes are wide, and she's hugging her arms tightly together.

"He probably thinks I'm a jerk now," Aggie says.

"No, he doesn't," I say, almost in a whisper. "He likes you, Aggie. And it's okay if you like him too. You liked him first. It's fine. I don't even know why I'm crying."

Aggie's jaw drops open and she just stares at me, shocked. "Cici," she begins, her voice low and quivering a bit now. But not like she's about to cry, more like she's . . . mad. "You're right. I did like him first. So why are you trying to make me feel bad?" she asks.

CHAPTER TWENTY-FIVE

"So you do like him?" I say accusingly. "Never mind. It's fine. I'll be fine. You guys make a great-looking couple."

"Yes, I mean, no. I mean, argh!" she says, angrily. "You're getting me all confused, Cici. Drew's nice. I like him as a person. He's the first boy at this stupid school not ogling me or making dumb jokes every time I walk into a room. And I like that he talks to me and not my boobs. That he's interested in hearing what I have to say. Yes, I like that, I like all of that."

She's yelling at me now. I glance at the door to see if anyone is coming out, but no one is. We're all alone outside.

"Yeah, I like Drew. I do. Just not in the way you're thinking. And he doesn't like *me*, Cici. He likes *you*. He just doesn't know it yet." She shakes her head, looking disgusted.

I swallow hard, not sure how to respond.

Aggie continues, not done yelling at me yet. "How am I supposed to feel when after one summer away I come back and everyone is treating me differently? Boys are giggling and staring at my chest. Girls are whispering nasty names under their breath when I walk by. And what did I do to deserve this? Drink too much milk? Hit a growth spurt? Even you act like I'm suddenly a different person just because I look a little different. When did I stop being Aggie and become an object?"

She kicks the ground and mutters, "At least in volleyball I can pull on two sports bras and stick out a little bit less."

"Two?" I ask.

"Not the point, Cici," Aggie says, annoyed.

She's right. I've been just as awful as everyone else at school and I was supposed to be helping her.

"Oh, Aggie," I say, "I'm so sorry. You're right. I haven't been a very good friend. I was totally wrong." I think back to what Claire had said that day at yoga. That best friends are hard to come by, but there will be many boys in my lifetime. I don't know if any of them will ever be like Drew but at this time, I've got to choose my friend. "In fact," I tell her, "I'm not going to talk to him either. I'll message him and tell him we can't talk anymore. That will end all of this. We're breaking up . . . whatever all of this has been."

She thinks about this. "Really?" she asks. "Are you sure?"

"I'm sure," I reply quickly before I can change my mind. "Can we just forget about all of it? Put it behind us?"

Aggie looks up in the air like she's thinking and then her face softens. "Yeah," she finally says. "Can we call your mom to pick us up, though? I don't want to go back in the gym. It's too awkward."

I nod. "Let's wait inside." I put an arm around her shoulder, and we head for the door.

26

Cici Reno @yogagirl4evr • 58 minutes ago
HALF MOON POSE - From Extended Triangle, bring right hand to the floor and straighten your right leg. Lift your left leg so that it is parallel to the floor. Reach toward the ceiling with your left hand and gaze upward. Helps you move on from what you thought was your true love.

Why did you run out like that?

I felt so stupid standing there.
All the guys were laughing at me.

What's with your last message? What do you mean you can't talk to me anymore?

Are you really not going to respond?

Helloooooooooo?

Is it because I kissed you?

I'm sorry. I shouldn't have done that.

Did I embarrass you?

Answer me, PLEASE.

D   Aggie?

That was the last message. It came in sometime around midnight, but I had already gone to sleep. Drew hasn't sent me any more messages. I think he's finally given up. I've reread these probably fifty times, but it doesn't change anything. It's over. I made my decision and I'm not going to talk to him again.

There's a knock at my bedroom door, and I quickly shut my computer. "Yes?"

"It's me," Mom calls.

"Come in."

"Everything okay, hon? You've been pretty mopey since you got home last night. Want to talk?"

"I'll be okay." I cross the room to my bed and plop down onto it.

Mom takes a seat next to me. "You and Aggie got into a fight, huh?"

I nod. "Everything's okay now. I guess I'm just still feeling a little sad about it, that's all."

Mom puts an arm around me and squeezes. "I used to hate fighting with friends when I was your age. It always felt like the end of the world. Like I couldn't see through the fight to the next day or week, you know? They were always this huge, overshadowing thing. But you know what, things always got better. It's okay to feel sad about it. Just know that you and Aggie will be fine, I promise."

"I hope so."

"Tell you what," Mom says, "let's cheer you up. How

about a girls' day? We can go out for lunch, maybe shop a bit? Let's get out of the house. Dad's taking the boys to a movie, and I'm not going into the studio until late this afternoon. What do you say?"

"The boys?" I ask.

"Yeah, Drew's over. He looks like he had a hard night too. How rough have middle school dances gotten anyway?" Mom says, heading for the door.

Oh man. I have to get out of here before Drew sees me. "Lunch and shopping would be perfect, Mom. Give me five minutes to get ready and we'll go."

"Great," Mom says. "I knew that would perk you up. And I need new boots, so that will perk me up too." She laughs. "Okay, see you in a few," she says, closing the door behind her.

I look at myself in the full-length mirror on the back of my door. I'm a mess. I rip off my old sweatpants and T-shirt and pull on a sweater and jeans. I brush my hair quickly and pull it up into a loose ponytail. I'm dabbing on lip gloss when there's a knock at my door again.

"Hold on, Mom," I yell. "Almost ready."

The door cracks open and Drew pops his head in. "I'm not your mom," he says. "Can I come in for a minute? I need to talk to you."

I'm frozen in place, lip gloss still in midair, totally freaking out. "Um, uh," I stammer, "yeah, sure. Come in."

Drew slips into my room, closing the door behind him. I can't believe this is really happening. That Drew Lancaster is in my room right now, just inches away.

"Um, what's up?" I ask him, backing away. I take a seat at my desk.

Drew nervously paces around my room. "Well," he begins and then pauses, hesitating. "I'm not sure how much you know." He stops pacing. "It's about Aggie."

I nod. "Yeah, Aggie. I do know about that."

"So you know that she's not talking to me anymore. That she doesn't want anything to do with me apparently. Only thing is, I don't know why. What did I do to suddenly make her so mad?"

This is so, so hard. Drew looks really hurt. I hate that I'm the reason he looks like this. "I'm sure you didn't do anything," I say quickly. "And I don't think she's mad. Not at all."

"She has to be," he says. "She wants nothing to do with me. I must have done something."

"No, it's not you, it's her," I say. That sounds so lame, like I got it off a TV drama or something. "I mean, Aggie's just not ready to date yet. Not anybody. It's nothing to do with you specifically. And she's really into volleyball right now and I think she just wants to concentrate on that, you know, with no distractions."

"Maybe I was coming on too strong. But I could have pulled back. It's not like we had to *date*, date. Honestly, I was happy just talking to her everyday online."

I smile and a tingly sensation shoots through me, right to my toes. He *does* like talking to me.

"Do you think you could try talking to her again for me? Maybe tell her I'm sorry and can we just be friends?" he asks. He looks so hopeful.

I sigh. "I don't think that's a good idea, Drew. She was pretty definite about this. I don't think talking to her will change things. No, I think the best thing you could do is let it be. Just move on and forget about her. Maybe . . . " I stop talking. Drew's not exactly paying attention to me. "Drew?" I ask.

Drew's eyebrows are furrowed and he's looking around my room, frowning. I follow his gaze from the laptop on my desk and the vampire gnome statue on my bookshelf to the pictures of The Stall all over my walls, from the light-up Yoda bank on my nightstand to my new Minecraft torch hanging up over my bed, and finally resting on my window, specifically on book five of *The Last Token*, tucked in between the screen and the glass.

Oh no.

Drew points his index finger at me and then pulls it back, biting his thumb. He drops his hand to his side and shakes his head. He looks like he's going to say something and then swallows hard. He turns toward my bedroom door.

"I—" I begin and stop. I have no clue what to say.

Drew whirls back around, angry now. "I've been talking to you this whole time?" he asks.

"Uh," is all I can get out so I give him a tiny nod.

"So, what," he says, sounding furious now, "you and

Aggie were playing some kind of joke on me? Making fun of me?"

"No," I reply quickly.

Drew just stares at me. He's so, so mad. But I can also see his eyes welling up and his jaw stiffen, like he's fighting to hold back tears.

I feel numb and lost. I don't know what I can say right now that will make any of this better.

"Well, I hope you two had a good laugh," he says quietly, before storming out of my room.

In all of that time of plotting and planning I never imagined this would happen. What did I do? My head falls into my hands. I think I'm in shock.

A second later, Luke is angrily stomping through my door and yelling, "What did you say to Drew to make him tear out of here like that?"

Luke is glaring at me, and I'm completely frozen. I can't respond.

This is so, so bad.

27

Cici Reno @yogagirl4evr • 29 minutes ago
KING COBRA POSE - Lie facedown. Place your hands flat on the floor, close to your chest, and lift up. Bend your legs up and try to touch your toes to the back of your head. Helps you to deal with the feeling of helplessness and makes you feel in power/control.

I threw up. Twice. And then I went shopping with Mom. I don't know how I got through it. I was basically robotic. I barely spoke a word. And I couldn't eat a thing at lunch. Mom's freaked out. She said she doesn't understand how I got more upset in the span of five minutes. But she doesn't know that in those five minutes I ruined absolutely everything. Drew hates me.

Mom drags me to yoga with her, and I don't put up a fight. Time to myself, an hour not having to talk to anyone or think about anything might be useful. Or I could become an even bigger mess.

"We're going to slowly move into Pigeon," Mom says in a soothing voice, slowly bringing the class to the end of our session. "Bring your right knee up the mat in front of you and put your toes of your right foot in front of your left knee. Find comfort in the uncomfortableness of this position."

Yeah, that's basically my life right now, I think. Trying to find comfort in the uncomfortable.

"When you're ready," she continues, "push your hands out to the front of your mat, place your head on the mat, and put your pigeon to sleep. We're going stay in this pose for a while. Find your comfort and keep breathing. A lot of emotions come out when doing this position. Don't try to hold them in, let them all out."

I feel myself choke back a sob. And then I'm crying, hard quiet tears, my shoulders are shaking. Everything is coming out.

I'm not sure how many minutes I sit in this position, but I can sense a shift of movement in the room, and I lift my head. The rest of the class is sitting in lotus, facing Mom. Thankfully, everyone still has their eyes closed, so they can't see what a mess I am. I wipe hard at my cheeks and face the front of the room.

"The light and the heart in me honors the light and the heart in you. Namaste," Mom says.

I place my palms together and slightly bow. "Namaste," I whisper in reply.

And suddenly I know what I'm going to do. I have to talk to Drew.

● ● ●

The next day our entire family loads into the car and heads for Luke's hockey game. My heart is racing at the thought of seeing Drew again, but it's inevitable. I'm going to have to see him at games and school and even at my house when he's hanging out with Luke. I can't avoid him forever, though that would be the easiest thing to do.

I have to be honest with him. I have to tell him everything and hope that he can forgive me. What other choice do I have?

I'm pacing back and forth near the penalty box, waiting for the guys to come out of the locker room and hit the ice for a pre-game warm-up. I left Mom and Dad in the stands. I told them I was going to get a hot chocolate, but the truth is, I've been barely able to eat or drink a thing since Drew confronted me yesterday.

I watch the team go out onto the ice, one by one. Even Luke's out there warming up, but I don't see Drew anywhere. Maybe he's hanging back because he sees me standing here next to the only door onto the ice on this side of the rink. Well, too bad. I'm not moving. He has no choice but to talk to me. A few more minutes pass, and then finally I see him. He's walking quickly toward the ice. I need to stop him fast.

"Drew, wait. Hold on a sec," I say. He almost gets by me and I reach out my hand and touch his shoulder. "Can you just wait? Just give me a minute to try and explain."

He stops, facing away from me, eyes on the rink. He doesn't turn around, but he doesn't go out on the ice either.

I guess this is the best I'm going to get. I take a deep breath.

"I know you have a game and I'm just going to say this quickly," I tell him. "I like you. A lot. But I couldn't tell you. Aggie technically liked you first and she asked for my help in getting your attention. She was too nervous to talk to you. So, I started talking to you online. For her. And the more I talked to you, the more *I* liked you."

I gulp. It looked like Drew flinched when I said that.

"And then," I force myself to continue, "Aggie said that she changed her mind and wasn't ready to date. And I wanted to tell you how I felt, but I know how things are. I know I'm not your type and probably never will be your type. Girls like Aggie are your type." I take another deep breath, trying to calm down. "But that didn't change how I felt. We hit it off so well online, and I don't know, maybe I thought that things could just go on like that forever. You'd never have to know SeraFrosted was me. You wouldn't take one look at me and reject me. You'd like me just for being me."

I pause. Drew doesn't move and he doesn't say a word. My eyes cast downward to the ground. He won't even look at me. Is he at least hearing me?

"Maybe it wasn't the greatest idea I ever came up with," I say. "And maybe things went too far. I probably never should have contacted you online in the first place. But if I hadn't, I never would have gotten to know you. Yeah, I started out talking for Aggie. But really, I was talking for me."

CHAPTER TWENTY-SEVEN

I glance at the ice. The game will be starting soon. I need to let him go.

"I know you're never going to talk to me again, Drew, and I understand. I wouldn't talk to me again either if I were you. I just wanted you to know, it was never a joke. *You* were never a joke to me. And I'm sorry. That's it."

I take a long breath, dizzy from the huge speech that just poured out of me. And I wait. And wait. Drew's not saying anything and he's not turning around.

Finally, he breaks his silence. Without looking at me, he says, "Doryan and Nylyan make it out of the forest okay. They find Driappi Bracegirdle's house. You can take book five out of time out."

"Oh," I say, taken aback. "Thanks. I will."

With that Drew pushes off onto the ice to warm up with the rest of the team.

Cici Reno @yogagirl4evr • 30 minutes ago
NAMASTE POSE - Sit cross-legged with your
hands in prayer in front of your heart, head bowed.
Helps clear your mind so you can find peace.

"**O**h, Cici! That was it? He didn't say anything else?"
Aggie asks as we sit across from each other at
Beanies, nursing vanilla frappés.

"Nope."

"You poured your heart out, and he just skated away?"

"Yeah. They lost the game 3-0 though, so he didn't play
very well," I tell her.

Aggie shakes her head, pursing her lips.

"It really doesn't bother you?" I ask her. "Me telling you
all this?"

"No, not at all," Aggie replies. "I mean, sure, I still think
he's cute but there never was like, a connection, between
us. I don't feel anything for him. Well, wait, I do feel anger
that he's brushing you off like this."

I can feel tears sting my eyes. Best. Friend. Ever. Instead of hating me too, Aggie's upset for me.

"And what was with the cryptic response about a stupid book?" she asks.

I smile. "It's not a stupid book. It's a great book. And that part was actually kinda sweet," I say.

"So, that's it then?"

"That's it," I say.

"You guys just go back to how it was before, just forget you ever had a connection," Aggie says.

"No, I can't forget. But nothing is going to happen, Aggie. I told you, I'm not his type. Boys don't fall for girls like me. They fall for girls like you. I always knew what the deal was."

"That's so lame. Boys suck," she says.

I shrug.

"Well, it's his loss. If he wants to be stupid like that, let him. You're a great person, Cici. And one day, guys will be lining up around the block waiting for a chance to date you."

"Thanks, Aggie." I get up and walk around the table and hug her.

● ● ●

Later that afternoon, I'm lying on the couch reading book five of *The Last Token* when there is a knock at the entryway. "I'm not hungry, Mom," I call.

Drew pops his head in the room. "Still not your mom. Do I have a real feminine knock or something?"

I scramble to sit up.

"Drew . . . " I say. I reach a hand up to smooth my hair, hoping I don't look too terrible.

He glances at my book and smiles. "So you took book five out of time out?"

I nod. "Doryan and Nylyan are still lost in the dark forest. He just made her a wedding ring out of some twigs in case they never find their way out."

I'm feeling really anxious and I don't know what to do with my hands, so I sit on them.

"Oh yeah, I like that part," he says.

"Me too."

He looks around. "Can I sit?"

"Yeah, sure." I motion to the cushion next to me.

It's more of a loveseat than a couch. When he sits, he's so close I can smell his spearmint gum.

My heart is racing. I pull a pillow onto my lap and hug it, trying to calm my nerves. I can see Drew's right leg bouncing, so he must be nervous too.

Drew takes a deep breath. "Thanks for telling me all of the stuff you told me at the game today."

"It was all true," I say.

"The thing is," he starts, "I'm not sure why you couldn't just tell me it was you talking to me online."

My eyes widen. "Really? I didn't think you'd ever take me seriously. I'm Luke Reno's little sister."

"I know that."

CHAPTER TWENTY-EIGHT

"I look like a little kid," I say, matter-of-factly.

"Yeah, me too," he replies.

I laugh. I know he knows what I mean, and he's just being nice. "Boys don't like me," I explain. "I'm not like Aggie."

"No, you're Cici."

We're both quiet.

"So . . . " I say.

"So," he repeats. "Maybe we can, like, I don't know, hang out sometime. Start talking online again."

"You sure you want to hang out with *me*?" I ask, unable to mask the surprise in my voice.

"Yes, SeraFrosted, I'm sure I want to hang out with you. What do you say?" he asks.

I feel like I couldn't stop smiling, even if I wanted to.

"I say . . . "

Because he has the worst timing in the world, Luke strolls into the living room, a bag of chips under his arm, a video game in one hand, a liter of pop in the other, and two cups under his chin. "Cici, out," he commands, coming straight for my seat. "We've got aliens to shoot."

I look at Drew. He catches my glance and quickly looks away. I'm still set to argue with Luke, but he warns, "I swear I will dump this whole thing of pop on you right now if you don't move."

● ● ●

I'm halfway up the stairs when my phone buzzes in my pocket. I'm so frustrated with Luke that I almost don't take it out. Almost.

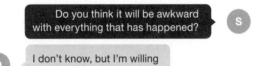

So, how about it? Can we hang out?

I'm instantly relieved but filled with butterflies. This is everything I've been wishing for, but what if he doesn't like me after all? What if he only thinks he likes me?

Do you think it will be awkward with everything that has happened?

I don't know, but I'm willing to take the chance.

I'm so nervous, I'm surprised I can even hold my phone.

Ok, DrewlingMess, me too.

ACKNOWLEDGMENTS

I'm incredibly grateful to the following wonderful people who've been a part of the making of this book:

My lovely agent, Andrea Somberg, for her wise thoughts, excellent advice, and for finding the perfect publishing home for *Cici*.

My dream editor, Brett Duquette, who understood and loved these characters as much as I did, offered great insight and guidance in making every part of the book better, and made the entire editing process a joy.

Hanna Otero, Hannah Reich, Merideth Harte, Andrea Miller, and the rest of the fantastic team at Sterling Children's Books.

• • •

My first-draft readers, longtime friends, and confidantes, Kristin Walker and Deena Viviani.

The yoga teachers at the Bolingbrook Park District, Breathe: The Art of Yoga, and the Naperville Fry's YMCA, for numerous hours of allowing me to study them (and not picking on my form).

The countless teachers, librarians, and booksellers (especially my dear hometown indie, Anderson's Bookshops) who have placed my books into so many readers' hands over the years.

My two sweet girls, Maya and London, for going to yoga with me and twisting into all the impossible poses I couldn't get into.

My parents, Jim and Gloria Voightmann; my brothers, Mark, Mike, and Bob; my kids, Teegan, Maya, London, and Gavin; and the rest of my family and friends, who have provided material for this book without realizing it. ;-)

My wonderful husband, Athens Springer, for his continuous love and support, and for being my number one fan always.

And finally, you, dear readers. Thank you for letting me share my stories with you.